MW00709953

ibo landing

ibo landing
an offering of short stories

ihsan bracy

cool grove press

Publisher's Cataloging in Publication Data

Bracy, Ihsan. 1953 –
    Ibo Landing : an offering of short stories
    / by Ihsan Bracy.
    p. cm.
    Preassigned LCCN: 97-077807
    ISBN Paper: 1-887276-10-6
    ISBN Cloth: 1-887276-11-4

    1. Gullahs—Sea Islands—Fiction. 2. Afro-Americans—
Sea Islands—Fiction. 3. Sea Islands—Fiction. 4. Afro-American
families—United States—Fiction. 5. Rural-urban migration—
United States—Fiction.
    I. Title

PS3552.R22I36 1998   813'.54
                                            QBI98-392

Front and back cover illustrations by Islah Alexander
Cover & book design: P. T. Hazarika
Author photo by Larry Brown
to prepare a way, restin' in and *ibo landing* were reprinted in
The Legacy of Ibo Landing, Clarity Press 1998

First Edition

Manufactured in the United States of America
First Edition: September 1998
10 9 8 7 6 5 4 3 2 1

our deepest fear is not that we are inadequate. our deepest fear is that we are powerful beyond measure. it is our light not our darkness that most frightens us! we ask ourselves, who am i to be brilliant, gorgeous, talented, fabulous? actually, who are you not to be? you are a child of god. your playing small doesn't serve the world. there's nothing enlightened about shrinking so that other people won't feel insecure around you. you are born to make manifest the glory of god that is within you. it's not just in some of us — it's in everyone. and as we let our own light shine, we unconsciously give other people permission to do the same. as we're liberated from our fear, our presence automatically liberates others.

— marianne williamson

*when i dare to be powerful —
to use my strength in the service of my vision,
then it becomes less and less important
whether i am afraid*

— audre lorde

for bunny, who was first to tell me
and the only one to listen

and

for aunt annie, whose gentle loving
was a sweetness which nurtures still

in memory of

justin **j**ohnson
(1984 — 1998)

and

dorothy **g**iles
(1922 — 1998)

all praises to the one, from whom all blessings flow.

offerings to the ancestors who allowed me to sketch a tale and often stayed for the telling.

ibo landing is given to my children zakiyyah, mustapha and jihad, with the prayer that it may bring them closer to the blessings of the ancestors.

a special thanks to my literary godmothers sherkaa osorio, sandra maria esteves and especially my editor, mentor and sister brenda connor-bey. words cannot express the depth of my gratitude. i will always be indebted to you. may the ancestors grant you peace. àláfià,

and a quiet thank you to all the spirits, guides and close friends who have been there for me.

you are appreciated.

orisha-nla

foreword

When speaking of a rich family heritage and what it means to its recipients, we think of them as being stronger in spirit and in mind because of stories passed from one generation to the next. We think of those people as having something solid to fall back on in times of need and we think of them, sometimes, with envy because they are in possesion of what holds a lineage together — living history.

ibo landing is a rich collection of short stories about ihsan bracy's family. This treasure box takes us from their torturous crossing out of Africa to the shores of South Carolina; from their migration from the southern United States to several northern cities. These stories tell tales of the kind of people many of us have heard about or perhaps dreamt of being ourselves. I know many women who, if they confronted their man in a sexual situation similar to that found by lizzie in *red rice and shrimps,* wished they had had the presence of mind to use the strong language or the strength to rectify the situation as she did!

In this retelling of his family stories, some of bracy's heroines ring faintly of Zora Neale Hurston's Janie who defied community and family and followed her dreams. And though ordinary, everyday folks, these are remarkable men and women whose love of family and tradition ring as clear as a bell calling folks to Sunday service.

I cannot speak for an entire nation of African Americans but I know many of us have had an aunt like the one in *warrior seed* who, "...was a terror," and who would, "...slap you in a minute. didn't care whose child you were. tell you she'd beat your mama, too, if she didn't like it." bracy's stories are lovingly placed before his readers as he celebrates the lives of these people. In the story *going home,* it is the testament to the life of matriarch, *mabel grey lee bertha fannie anne lou ella may franklin lewis,* a woman that "the heart chakra had been hers to command — her enormous capacity to love."

There is myth and magic in this wonderful book and you will find yourself nodding your head in wonder, appreciation and approval as you savor each story. It will be a book you will open many times as you look among its characters for reaffirmation of a childhood gone or friendships and loves lost. It will linger in your memory as it has in that of ihsan bracy and we should thank him for remembering.

— Brenda Connor-Bey, July, 1998

preface

ancestral voices, whisper tales which demand to be told.

there were two major ports of entry for the amerikan slave trade, one centered around charleston, south carolina and one in norfolk, virginia.

captured, transported but never enslaved, my father's people came in through south carolina, during the beginnings of the civil war. in south carolina slaves were first landed on the coastal sea islands, to be cleaned, fattened and prepared for the auction block. cargo landed after the civil war had begun was declared free after the civil war was lost. these people, originally thought to be from angola, were called gullah. it is now believed that they may have come from sierra leone.

remaining isolated on the islands, the people maintained much of their cosmology and some of their language. eventually they moved off the sea islands and made a slow migration onto the mainland. those who left the sea islands were called geechee. my father's people made it as far as summerville, eleven miles away from charleston and there most remain.

my mother's family came in through virginia and were moved across to staunton, a shanandoah valley town in the central western part of the state, in the blue ridge mountains.

the distance from the coast made slave purchasing difficult. many times communities would buy slaves from the same ship, consequently populating areas with slaves from neighboring lands. this helped maintain some vestiges of tradition. once slaves arrived in a mountainous or remote region, they rarely left it.

as time passed, my mother's family spread out, mostly across the northeastern seacoast.

my parents, both born in the south, met in new york city. they married and conceived me in harlem. although raised in new york city, i was born in the blue ridge mountains of my ancestors.

the ancestral voices which call out from ibo landing tell stories of my family, through six generations. for the most part they are told in genealogical order and as is the way of ancestor tales, for the most part they are true.

— ihsan

the time before this

ibo landing

restin' in

red rice & shrimp

to prepare a way

sandwich

cherry

old man's sport

abominable snowman

crossing the river

warrior seed

ring-o-levio

fifty/fifty

sister/sister

coming upon malcolm

done

proposal

bubble gum

angels?

going home

across

blue pearl

table of contents

prologue

the time before this

for buddy, addio, herbie, juan, jorge, sandy, don juan, earl, lincoln, gary, sin se, yancy, bobby, foster, aaron, eli, ivan, wizard angel and forever child

running. smooth elongated strides, running uphill, full out, extending, stretching for every second, reaching for every piece of land. power running, the trained physique in rhythm, sweat pouring down like sunshine in the humid savannah morning. running with assuredness, with the knowledge of all the years of training, with the responsibility, trust, safety and perhaps survival of the people, of all they have ever known.

spirit running. connected to the circle of spirit warriors, sent out in every direction, the ever widening ripple carrying the message, following the call first sent out on drums.

time running. running for time. time of the utmost importance. there had never been a time so important. remembering the call sent out on drums, a rhythm heard only once before; recalling the voice of the elder who explained the significance of this particular rhythm underlined again the importance of his mission.

hearing heart pounding running, settling down to running within the rhythms of the sounds within and without. seeing all the spirit warriors around the fire, hearing on the drum, *they've landed, they're here!!!*

memory running, over footpaths familiar, worn smooth through childhood footprints and run as they had been during manhood training.

clearing the set of trees at the top of a hill, becoming aware of the unnatural silence of the jungle, the warrior son stopped instinctively. these were dangerous times. although speed was demanded, caution was due. his keen eyesight had only to focus on the expanse to notice the movement. it took only a moment longer to see the invading ghosts.

as the warrior son moved against the closest trees, he was struck, even at this distance, by the awkwardness of their movements and the whiteness of their skins. clumsy ghosts cutting their way through jungle, rather than walking footpaths that to him were so apparent.

he knew he could no longer continue on this footpath, it careened down the side of the clearing and would expose him to the apparition which he was witnessing. calling upon the strength of ancestors who had never seemed closer, the warrior son turned toward the marshy lands of the coast for cover and proceeded to make his way along the border of trees, determined to complete his mission. it was hard for him to reconcile the horror which he had witnessed, the blight which had been visited upon his life, land and the existence of the people.

he was moving too quickly through unfamiliar areas, near panic running. he had seen with his own eyes the source of their violation and now the possibility of horrors speculated were more real and the desperation felt to complete his mission even greater.

suddenly the warrior son realized he was the only defense between the invading ghosts and his village. he turned. warrior son went into battle position and began chanting to the ancestors.

the spirit warrior stood next to a hugh baobao tree, praying. the ancestors listened. they would not allow the purity of his fire to be touched by defilers. they would relinquish neither son or spirit into enslavement.

as the warrior son stood to meet the invading ghosts he raised his spear. double lightning reached down from sky connecting ancestor and spear, reclaiming warrior son and spirit as the invading ghosts were felled by the burning tree.

★ ★ ★

sea islands

ibo landing
for ivor

they would not remove themselves from his mind.

he dreamt of them, of her, every night. they all did.

the mass of human flesh lay beached upon the shore. in the pale early dawn they were indistinguishable.

they were poured upon the sands, fished out of nets like pounds of shrimp.

as his eyes adjusted to the light, he could make out land. he wondered, as he watched the ghosts move about, to what special hell he had been brought.

he would never forget the sound of teeth gnashing as she gave herself to the sea.

––––––––

she gave herself to the sea. there was no struggle. she sensed him behind her. she reached back as his hand found hers. she squeezed it tight. she had only time to grab him before being engulfed by water.

––––––––

razzberry heard the unloading all night. as the sun began to rise, he could make out the mound of brown human flesh on the shore and the shadow of the ship beyond.

----

he could feel people all around him. he had grown use to this communal form. he had lost the parameters of his own body, just as he had given up the designs of his soul. it took all his effort to open his eyes. for so long it had seemed so useless, confined to the shadows and darkness as he had been.

ghosts moved about freely, unconcerned for their cargo. there was the sense of exhilaration and completion that came at the end of each journey. satisfaction, having delivered over half of their cargo safely. they waited for the auction and the payment of their money.

as the sun rose, the mound began to move. warmed as they were by the sun, they no longer clung to each other. as the thaw of the journey and last night's unloading set in, the cold subsided. they each began to take back their limbs.

they all remembered kiobe's screams, among those of the other women the ghost had chosen.

----

kiobe had been taken for the longest, passed around as she was. no one had seen her for two risings of the moon. they had begun to think of her as lost when she returned bloody, taken, wet with the pollution of many ghosts. she cried until she fell asleep, then she screamed until she woke herself to cry.

——————————

atiba saw her from one corner of the vessel. she saw him. he saw it in the look in her eyes. she knew it in his. by the time he reached the railing she had already leaped. he focused on where the waters had withdrawn her. he eluded the hands of many ghosts reaching. he jumped after.

sharks that followed the ship of death continued in the process of their evolution, cleaning the waste and filth, drawn as they were by the blood of her taking and the remains of the communal blood in which they had lain.

they all remembered. it would not escape their dreams.

——————————

slowly they returned to life. scared. scarred by the passage. they had crossed. they were the bridge. generations would cross through their collective womb.

each in their own way understood the distance. they would never again be home.

there were many tongues, many peoples among them. most were still chained. slowly they were released into a pen, washed, clothed, then given some gruel to eat, passed by ladle, by ghosts, from one communal pail.

as they were released they drifted together in the communal pen.
it was here that for the first time many of them were able to find
the sister tongues they had heard in the darkness.

----

that darkness. lying one upon the other. barely breathing.
constant endless shifting, in the struggle for room. all would
not survive. it had seemed an eternity before the one voice
called out for silence. those of his tongue indicated this to
each who was near. in this way slowly the silence had been
achieved.

calling the name of a people, those of that tongue would cry
out searching for information: a sound, a name, a place, anything familiar, any vestige of their ever distancing home.

it was on that day, when a young warrior son urged the people to learn the sounds of the one in bondage beside them
that resistance was born. resistance which gave birth to survival.

so many died. so many gave themselves to the sea.

----

amazingly the eyes adapted to the darkness, to whatever
little light surrendered itself through the virtually non-exis-
tent openings in the belly of the wooden ship.

next had come the arduous task of moving. each day at least
one shift. as the voyage continued there had been more
room.

there had been death, left to rot amongst them. they had lost
so many. fluids everywhere, from every opening of the
living, the dying and the dead. this was the constant in
which they survived.

one quarter of the cargo was brought above each day. fed.
drenched in the waters of the sea, made to move, dance, then
returned to the constant. the methodology developed by the
success of many crossings.

----

among them were a people who did not speak.

the people of the silence could hear the thoughts of one
another. they alone knew the fate in each cargo hold.

atiba had known each of kiobe's thoughts, through every
scream. they all had.

----

they waited until the washing was complete. the morning
moon watched. silently they turned and began walking back
toward the water.

movement was undetected for several minutes. their guard was down. they had passed the night. the cargo had been washed, fed, clothed and penned. auction was set for high sun.

the pens were guarded heaviest on the sides near the woods, near where the auction would take place. the slavers held the hill overlooking their prized cargo. it was a while before they noticed the silent band of thirty or more moving without hesitation toward the waters.

----

as they reached the limits of the pen they jumped it as one. they turned not a head, even as the sounds of agitation grew behind them. they quickly crossed the distance of the natural harbor.

----

the slavers were stunned. cautious, they sprang into action. quickly they realized they could cut off every path except the one which led to the water. they reached for their guns, but were confused, fearful to injure even a single piece of cargo if it could be helped. suddenly angry, they contemplated their loss.

as if breaking out of a dream state, the slavers suddenly broke into a panicked run, each cursing non-stop, blaspheming their god and their luck. then they suddenly stopped, silenced by what they saw but could not comprehend.

razzberry watched from the hill. it was through him the story was remembered and the truth told.

as they reached the place of waves, each one would grab the hand of the one before.

stepping over wave after wave, they strode confidently, unhurriedly, past the ship lying in the sunrise.

----

nearly everyone in the vicinity of ibo landing that day came to see, before the silent band was lost from sight.

★ ★ ★

restin' in

for ida raspberry

by the time the family arrived back from the funeral she was
packed. she sat on the edge of the quilt covered bed to sur-
vey her handiwork. there were rows of cardboard boxes, all
lined up against the faded flowered papered walls. every item
of her life was labeled, categorized and dispensed with. there
was a sense of completion, finality. she had neatly emptied
out her closets first, then the bureau chest of drawers, one
drawer at a time, starting at the bottom. she had been surprised how amazingly simple it had all been, how little effort
it had all taken, how quickly it had all been accomplished. all
of one's life, wrapped up so easily. she could hear the stirring
of the womenfolk downstairs in the kitchen, quietly
preparing ever-flowing food, ready for people when they
returned. she heard the continual answering of the door
with the arrival of the many plates and offers of condolences.

she had not gone to the funeral. had not been invited, as it
were. she wondered how it was that her family could think
that just because she had lived as long as she had that suddenly she wouldn't be able to stand things. she had stood all
of them, for all those years. had borne nine children, eleven
if you count the two that had died at birth. well really only

one had died, in her arms; the other had laid still as they
pulled him from her. a beautiful boy, her first child, perfectly formed in every way 'cept for the purple cord wound
tight around his neck. he was a deep brown color, dead.

she had neatly folded away all the clothes of her life, except
for what she was wearing, the night clothes laid out on her
bed and the gold and white dress which hung on the door
of the closet. folded and packed all of her clothes, memories
still clinging to them each. as she folded she caught trails of
memory here, floods of remembrances there. the summer
whites had reminded her of over a century of conversations
among the womenfolk. births, pregnancies, adulteries,
comings and goings whispered from each and every crease.
faces. faces that came back without names. names that had
been carried along by the wind. wind carried along with
the footprints of a country road's dusty life.

she had neatly folded away all of her clothes, according to
their function. summer clothes together, a line of fall, winter, spring coats hung quietly above shoes that had walked
the miles of a lifetime. miles uphill, downhill, wet or dry.
snow storm miles, summer shine miles, pregnant miles,
carrying in the arms miles, tugged and cried after miles and
the calling, calling, calling of her name, sweet master! folded neat piles of house dresses, given to her over the years and
the box full of the ever present white aprons, the uniform of
her old age which she had worn dutifully, had taken for a
widow's veil. except for church going she had not been seen
out of one for more than forty years or at least as long as
anyone's memory.

from her window she noticed the dust rising from the lane and realized the clan had returned. she looked around one last time, inspecting the room for any last item that needed to be attended to. satisfied that her work was done, she started down the stairs, silently assured with the knowledge that she was indeed ready for her journey.

she arrived at the bottom step just as the door swung open and one of her more than twenty-six grand, nineteen great-grand eleven great great-grandchildren and six great great great-grandchildren hit the door, tearing at the tie around his neck. the top button of his too starched white collared shirt had torn at him, tormenting him throughout the entire service. she had just sat in her chair when the chorus of

-hi mam mam,

echoed through the room.

-gwine tell you granddadi i wan' fuh see e,

she said quietly to one of the twins as they passed within earshot. they both ran off together to see who could find their grandfather first, each wanting to be the one to bring her summons.

grand geechee was just stepping from the limousine when he saw his twin grandsons racing toward him.

-mam mam wan' fuh see you,

they both said in unison. as he walked slowly toward the
front porch of the house he had known all of his life he
remembered running as a child like he now saw his grandsons do.

he had just come back from burying him, his father, her son.
her last remaining child. he could almost see his father
standing, leaning on the porch, looking out as he had so
often. he had been in favor of telling her but had been dis-
suaded by the voices of all his sisters worrying that she
wouldn't be able to take it. he had argued that she had over-
seen the coming in and going out of each and every one of
them. the sisters had countered with how they all knew that
benjamin had been her favorite, her youngest.

-e gwine tek it hard,

had echoed throughout the family. against his better judg-
ment he had sat by as everyone was instructed

-not tuh tell mam mam,

convincing themselves that at her age it would be best. as if
they couldn't recognize that she had known everything that
had happened in each of their lives, always, without anyone
having told her most of anything.

she had buried two husbands, now eleven children and she
was as close to the grave as she ever hoped to be. she had
lived well past a century, a hundred and twelve or thirteen,

waiting for her time, looking toward the release which had
been promised her, which would signal the reward for all her
service. she had seen so much of life her eyes were tired of
looking. had seen wars, so called spanish wars, world wars,
wars in places called korea and vietnam. had seen people
ride out on the horse and buggy and come back from the
moon. had danced in front of soldiers in gray marching out
to a civil war. she had been barefooted, just a dusty dress
standing in a dusty road. they had marched out in lines
stretching out for most of a day. she had watched the not so
many come back, broken, battered, beaten into ruins, chased
by the long line of blue uniforms which signaled her release.
she had seen crosses burnt and people hung from trees left to
rot. she had lived from slavery to segregation, through
segregation to integration, from nigger to negra to negro to
colored to black. she was the stuff they spoke of when they
said,

-dey don' mek 'em li'e dey use tuh.

she still had her health, she still had her life. she still ran the
house, cooked every breakfast and oversaw the cooking of
every meal. she walked the half mile down hill every day to
the mailbox and back up. she usually strolled down to call
on miss bernice to sit and pass a little time whenever
weather permitted, until miss bernice had passed a little more
than four years ago.

she had outlived all of her friends and almost everyone she
had ever met throughout her life, all the children of her

friends and some of their grandchildren. even past the burial of her baby benjamin whom they had put away today. didn't nobody have to tell her that benjamin was gone. she had known it. had seen it all before it happened. she alone had seen the darkness that was closing to engulf the last of the babies she had pushed from her womb. she had been four or five years old when she had seen the soldiers first march and that made her at least old enough to sit on the front pew to mourn the passing of her last child.

she had already said goodbye to benjamin, when he left the night before last. had pulled him to her, hugged him close in her arms for what she knew would be the last time. what messages she wanted sent on to her loved ones on the other side were tucked softly and carefully behind the folds of his soul. not a heavy weight to carry, just a little message that she would be coming soon.

she had never been sick a day in her life, not even a child-hood disease. the doctor had told her she was a medical mar-vel and that she should leave her body to science. she had paid him no attention because she knew she was leaving her soul to the lord and all that came with it.

she had not slept a sunrise, except counting a few rises after early morning births. she smiled, remembering the look in benjamin's eyes the first time she held him. he had given her the least trouble of all. had been the easiest birth, as if he couldn't wait to jump from her loins to embrace life. maybe that was why she loved him the most. he gave her the least amount of trouble throughout his life too. he had been the child most like her, quiet, always with that sullen look. she remembered the eyes of the first child, the one born still. she suddenly knew that she was tired, very tired, as tired as she had ever felt. yet at the same time she felt this feeling of being light, excited, like a young girl on her first overnight stay.

grand geechee came into the room.

-no nee fuh hol' down you head.
i 'no benj'mn duh gwine.
'no y'all duh bury i las' chile,
duh put e en da groun'.
i nee fuh talk you, tuh all yous.
i nee fuh look on ewa one i chi'ren
y'all come on in chere.

she had never called for a meeting of the entire clan before. she answered the eyebrows of surprise that grand geechee raised by sitting back, looking out the window. he understood that she would not speak again until they had all assembled.

after they had all gathered into the living room, she turned her gaze from the tree outside and the path of the setting sun. she let it fall on the fruit of her womb. the tree of her life had been fertile and the collection of beauty that she confronted made her feel proud. she knew that both fathers of these children were feeling pride wherever they were at the evidence of their seed and its strength.

she looked at them all. they were a good looking family, ebony colored, to a child. blessed with the same tender smiles of their grandfathers and the loving eyes and spirits of their grandmothers. they were the proof of her existence, of a life well spent on this earth. she took a moment to look into each pair of eyes and in that space found time to love each and every one of their spirits as she gave them the blessings of her life. she took from each of them as much of their earthly weight as she could carry, quietly cleansing each and every one of them in the process. when this task had been completed she looked out and began in a voice clear with thoughts concise,

-i a scrong 'oman, dere ain' no nee fuh trea' i a chile.
i olda dan 'mos' two, tree a fuh a yous.
i 'no benj'mn duh dead.
see' e gwine fuh da bus en buy e a tickit e
won' nebwa use. saw benj'mn lay out en
e blue suit ewar 'fuh e leawe dis house.

they all looked around, the younger ones surprised. grand geechee just shook his head at the futility of their attempt to hide benjamin's death from mam mam.

-saw anna margret in e blue hat wid da weil,
dat mousy look 'roun' e mout' e get whenewa e
'bout tuh cry.

but dat ain' 'hy i duh call you chi'ren tuhgeda.
i a old 'oman. so old cyan't 'zactly cyall i age.
i duh birt' i nine lit'le brown babi en duh see
dem tru. now all i babi gwine down, down en da quiet
eart'. i finish. i job duh duh.

she silenced the cries of

-oh mam mam

with a wave of the hand.

-now y'all list'n tuh i. i finish. i duh duh, tru.
i tired. i duh raise dis chere fam'li,
duh cyarried y'all dis long way, a slawery times tuh
ri' chere. i lord duh see' i tru da passin' a i trial en
tribuashun. now i glory time duh cyome.

again there began the beginnings of an outcry which she
silenced with one line,

-i bag duh pac', i time duh cyome!
i leawin' here 'fuh mawnin sun.
now y'all cyome on up en giwe mam mam
hugs en some sugah,

and with that she picked up her youngest great great-granddaughter and enfolded her into her arms.

there was not a sound. the members of the family just
looked around at each other, not knowing exactly what to

say or do. the words she had just spoken remained. not just because of what she had said, but because each of them realized in their own way how much she had loved them and they her. for as long as anyone could remember mam mam had never spoken a word that was not truth. not just that she didn't lie, but anything that she had ever said always came true. she knew about benjamin as she had known about her first husband little. knew even before he went possum hunting that night that the white men would be hunting him. knew that he wouldn't return. she had tried to stop him, but he wouldn't listen. after he had gone she had simply taken out her black mourning shawl, thrown it over her shoulders and had sat by the window all night and rocked, waiting. she had been sitting rocking the next morning when they had brought his body home on the back of his wagon, the rope still knotted around his neck, as it had been when the tree stump which held its other end had not given as the weight choked the life out of his body. she had always known things. a conjure woman some of her neighbor womenfolk would say, behind her back, when she was out of earshot. even then they were sure to whisper, never hurt to be safe, but as the years had worn on nobody could remember anyone being anything but helped by her gifts, so they were spoken of less and less, until they were forgotten or the secret had itself gone to the grave with the secret keepers.

as she hugged each of her grand, great-grand and great great-grandchildren she gave them each instructions, final directions and advice. this one was to make sure she stayed away from salt, this one was to leave the sugar alone. this one was to keep his wife from doing too much when her time came and she should name the boy after her father. she told the womenfolk who was to get what box, to see to it that miss so and so was to get this or that and to please keep so and so away from her room and out of her medicine chest. she told which boxes were marked with the things she had left for each of them.

after the dispensation of all her worldly goods was detailed and repeated back to her satisfaction she kissed each of them. then she sat each of the babies on her lap and talked to them one at a time.

when she had finished giving away all her blessings she had nothing left but her smile. slowly she stood and walked to the doorway that led to the stairs and the rooms above. she turned to the eyes within the ebony faces and gave away her final smile.

> -now y'all 'memba all 'hat i duh teac' yous.
> y'all 'memba fuh lovwe one 'notha.
> y'all 'memba 'here yous duh cyome a
> en 'hat yous duh cyome tru.
> y'all 'member dat yous a all yous hab. cherish
> each 'notha. 'memba dat all a y'all a sronga dan any one
> of yous 'lone. no, now don' star' fuh cry. hush up dat noise,
> y'all hear?

she said in response to some who were beginning to beg her not to go,

-i duh liwed i life, more dan. i duh tired, finish!
now y'all got fuh let i go. i wisit duh tru.

now mr. waughn down tuh trin'ty 'no all dere fuh 'no
'bout puttin' i 'way. now i don' wan' yous fussin'
en hollerin' en moanin' ower i en such, y'all hear?
list'n now, i tell yous. it ain dignify fuh chastise
da lord 'hen e duh giwe i so much alre'dy. ooouuu!

she stretched,

-i duh so tired i hardly cyan kee' i eye open,
but i 'clare 'fuh da lord i god, cyome tuhmorra mawnin
i's gwine be wadin' tru da riwer 'cross da distan' sho',
in i fada's house. da boat man a duh cyome for i en
i don' aim fuh kee' e wait not a momen longa.
i cyan 'mos see da green of da mount'n on da oda si'.
i reward time fuh duh cyome en at las' i gwine
drink a da gold'n cyup a ease.

slowly she turned and ascended the stairs this last time. they
could hear her singing every so softly,

-swee' swee' chariot cyomin', cyome fuh cyarry i home.

after she retired there was a stillness around the house that
just couldn't be shaken. finally after a while the great-great-
grandchildren slept. one by one so did the great-grandchildren and finally the grand. grand geechee was the last to fall
into a fitful sleep. only the youngest of the children slept
well that night.

the youngest great-granddaughter was the first to wake, rising with the sun. she tipped into her great-grandmother's room to see if she had indeed left on her journey. as her eyes grew accustomed to the early morning light which rushed through the curtained window she noticed the immaculately clean room. her great-grandmother lay there, perfectly still, as still as the boxes alongside the walls or the fall, winter and spring coats hanging quietly above the silent shoes and their silent miles.

she tiptoed up to the bed to peer into the face of tranquility on the body which seemed so shrunken and small underneath the quilted bedspread. she recognized the smile on the face of the body which had just contained the spirit of her great-grandmother, but what she noticed most was the sense of calm, peace and completion on the ageless face. she looked like she was resting. so peaceful. the great-granddaughter realized that indeed she had gone.

she tiptoed down the steps to tell the others that they had better not wait. that they had better fix breakfast this morning for themselves. mam mam would not be coming down today. she was restin' in.

★ ★ ★

red rice and shrimp
for bebop

lizzie came down the path with a purpose. she was going to her man. her heart thumped just about loud enough for anybody within a few feet to hear. in her hand she carried the brown paper bag in which she had neatly wrapped and placed the lunch of red rice and shrimp she had so lovingly prepared.

she knew it was his favorite. she had been to the market early. had sought out the shrimpers and had chosen carefully, one at a time, four pounds of the best looking shrimp to be found anywhere in south carolina. her studied catch wrapped and under one arm, she headed home. from her garden she picked the tomatoes, onions and green peppers she would need. after she sautéed the onions and peppers added to the tomatoes to make her sauce, she ceremonially washed and cleaned the shrimp. she created the traditional dish with a patience born out of love.

she cut a striking figure, this pretty black woman who could freeze you with a stare. she walked with a gliding stride, deceptively fast. she carried herself with the dignity of the ancestor gullah and in the seductive sway of her hips men

were returned to the shores of their forefathers. head up,
back straight, eyes focused, alert, defiant, strong willed, she
moved with grace, beauty and strength. she was always
dressed impeccably, in the height of style. she would not
leave the house unless she looked her best. this she had
learned from her father, the grand geechee. on her feet were
brand new brown leather button up heels. effortlessly she
moved. around her was such a stillness that even the dust
from the road refused to settle on those brand new brown
leather button up heels.

as she came in sight of her husband's shoe repair shop, her
chest filled with pride. there were not many colored men
who owned their own business in this little town. besides
the shoe repair shop there was only the barbershop, the
blacksmith, the dressmaker, the candy and hardware stores.
there was something nice about owning something of your
own. she approached the front steps of the shop. she was
met by the clerk, on his way to an errand he never left for.
she noticed that he was unusually talkative this afternoon, all
about the weather and goings on in the town. this from a
man who had hardly said more than

                            -good day

for the four years she had known him. he appeared agitated.
he was dressed in his shop apron. brush in hands and tools
still around his waist, he seemed somehow unprepared to be
leaving. she was pressed to be able to extricate herself from
this uncharacteristically long-winded discourse. finally she

simply excused herself, continuing on into the shop, determined to deliver the red rice and shrimp while it was still warm. she had an appointment to be fitted early this afternoon for a new dress she planned to wear for their seventh anniversary party next month. it was to be a surprise. she wanted always to look good for her husband because he so appreciated it. his eyes would fill with pride and his chest would just sit out as he took her arm whenever he escorted her anywhere.

-lizzie,

he would say as he appraised her from head to toe,

-if yuh ain' 'bout da fines' 'oman
dat god duh see' fit tuh put breat' inta,

and she would just beam as she allowed herself to be guided by his hand into a room.

her eyes had barely adjusted to the relative darkness of the store when she heard the noise coming from the back room. she heard unmistakably familiar moans and pants as she moved toward the door, as well as the puppy yells of some bitch in heat. the door was ajar. she could see her husband's shoes, toes pointed upwards. she slowly pushed open the door.

all she saw was this yellow backside about to lower itself upon her temple of blackness. lizzie said not a word. all that was heard was the yelp of surprise as lizzie brought her right foot back and then tried with all her might to part that yellow backside as moses had parted the red sea. she planted the toe of that brand new brown leather button up heel halfway up the crack of that yellow behind. as the brand new brown leather button up heel met its mark, lizzie opened up her mouth. she could be heard as far away as the barbershop, the hardware store, the blacksmith and the dressmaker at the end of the dirt road or the candy store across the street. the sound of lizzie's tirade brought everyone within earshot at least a few steps closer to her voice.

-don' yuh dare move downward, not one inch!
bitch, if yuh don' get ya rhiney yella
ass up off my husband 'fuh i kill ya ri' here! ya blazon,
no good yella hussy heifer, i'll skin ya 'live
a fuh i'm through, as god's true, as e is my witness,
i will today! lit'le bitch en heat, lying down wid
ewery dog come ya way! get up, so i can knock
ya skinny hi' yella behind down!

lizzie had, in one motion, put the bag with the red rice and shrimp down and unbuttoned one of the brand new brown leather button up heels. she took it off and spun it around. with the brand new brown leather button up heel she began to beat out a rhythm of no return on the girl's yellow behind and face.

after the initial contact, the girl tried to gather her clothes but lizzie was having none of it. she rained terror down on the yellow girl and finally drove her barefoot and bare-assed into the street with only her slip held in front of her as she ran down the front steps of the store past the growing group of interested faces. lizzie was not a second off her behind.

-run ya blazon yella heifer hussy, run!
'cause if i catch ya i'll kill you!
run on, looking like jus' 'hat ya are! trash!
ain' mo' dan a cat en heat! well go on en find yaself another
lickin' stick,
'cause ain' nobody sitting here but me
let me catch ya 'round here sniffin' again,
and i'll hab someding for ya!
'cause ain' nobody sittin' here but me!

lizzie said not another word. she didn't even bother to give her husband a look. quietly she put on her brand new brown leather button up heel. quietly she buttoned it. quietly she picked up the package of red rice and shrimp and tossed it into the garbage can near the door. quietly she turned and walked, head erect, eyes front, past the number of people in the street. quietly she walked defiantly up the path to her house and proceeded to pack. just as quietly she walked out of his life.

when her husband returned home that evening, flowers and candy in hand, lizzie was nowhere to be found. when the flowers had dried, withered, turned brown and crumbled, he realized she was gone forever.

from that day on lizzie was a different woman. she left the

south and moved up north. she would find another man to love but she would never visit him at work and she would never again fix red rice and shrimp.

★ ★ ★

to prepare a way
for alex

-herman!
hey you herman!
where is that boy?
herman! i say herman! you hear me?
herman! you hear me calling you boy?
herman!

-ma'am? coming ma'am. yes ma'am?

called the sandy red haired boy as he ran up to the porch dressed in faded patched overalls, pieces of dried grass sticking to the back of his plaid work shirt. the color of his hair matched the color of the dust flying up behind him as well as the color of the setting sun. he had been playing with one of his younger brothers, hiding under a pile of wood in the shed out back of the house when he heard his mama's call.

-boy, walk your grandma home.

-yes ma'am.

-and don't stop to pick no blackberries!

-no ma'am.

-snakes get you up in there after dark.

it was nearing dusk. the moon hadn't yet risen over the country road. the boy, who was nearly ten, took his grandmother's arm as they started down the steps of the porch. the boy always looked forward to this walk. he enjoyed any time spent away from the constant chores of the farm. he loved to explore, his favorite activity. he knew most of the county like the back of his hand.

his grandmother shook herself free of him as they started down the path that ran near the mill brook. although she was nearly ten times his age, he was still hard pressed to keep up with her determined step as she allowed her stride to open up. he fell in behind her. as they approached the little foot-bridge that crossed over the brook his grandmother remarked how low and still the water was for this time of year. the path then took them through the clump of woods where the blackberries grew buckwild. they were so ripe the boy could smell them. he had gotten sick more than a few times, unable to tear himself away from the sweetness of nature's charms. the path took them past the old church grounds and the old graveyard where his grandfather and his grandmother's other husband were both buried.

the moon was beginning to rise. as it began to grow darker the boy had no fear of the return trip for he had practically grown up in these woods. there was little he didn't know about them. by the time they reached the fork in the road, the moon had barely risen above the edge of the trees.

this was a familiar walk to his grandmother's cabin. she had lived way back, out in the bosom of the woods for as long as he had known her. the family had tried to get her to move in with one of her children or grandchildren after her last husband had died. lord knows she had enough family, but she had been adamant in her determination to remain in her little cabin in the woods. she refused to be a burden to anyone, she had argued. besides, she didn't have a need to see them everyday. so when his grandmother came to visit two or three times a week, he always walked her back home. his brothers would complain if asked, but he enjoyed these walks and their talks. his grandmother would sometimes walk for miles without saying a word, then she might make one small comment which would have him thinking for the rest of the week. there were times when she could be so quiet, then there were times when she would be so full of stories that they would already be at her cabin and he nearly back home before he stopped laughing. he looked forward to these times. it gave him a sense of closeness, being alone with his grandmother and he loved not sharing her with all of his brothers and sisters. he had no way of knowing how meaningful these walks were to her.

> -tell herman to come on and walk his poor granny
> home.

> -that boy will be the death of me yet,

his mother would complain,

-don't be so hard on my baby, now. he ain't nothing but
a child.

-hard. i need to crack his behind more often.

-you leave my baby alone now.

-leave him alone? humff! that's what's wrong with him now.

-he's my baby.

-and you can have him.

-that boy gonna be the flowering of your old age.

-if he ain't the death of me. gonna put me in my grave.

-that boy got the sight.

-he got the devil in him, that's for sure.

-i'clare, he mind me of my virgil, that's for sure,
when he was 'round about that age.
he was that way, strong-willed, followed his own mind.

she would laugh, remembering.

-got his behind whipped more than a few times too.
herman strong like him too.
and the boy got the gift.
i known it from time i first held him in my arms.

she was referring to the mark, the white tuft of hair at the top of his head that had been there at birth. the mark moved down through one eyebrow and would eventually pass through the mustache and beard that he would one day grow. she could see in him evidence of signs she had first recognized in herself. signs she had looked for, in vain, in every child and grandchild that had been presented to her until she had nearly given up. she had finally found satisfaction in the strong brown eyes of the sandy red haired bundle she had been handed on that cold april night. it was after she heard the first cry of this her seventh grandchild that she had looked out the window to see the disappearing moon. the fact that he had been born during a total eclipse of the full moon only confirmed the signs dreamt of and the ones she had already witnessed in his eyes.

this night, as they approached the bend in the road that signaled the beginning of his grandmother's land, he heard a strange sound coming towards them. a creaking kind of sound, at first, something that sounded like a wagon wheel needing oiling. then the clump clump clumping of a mule drawn wagon ahead. he looked around but could see nothing. he strained his eyes and ears in the direction of the oncoming wagon, but still he could see only the darkness surrounding them. he wondered how it was even possible for a mule drawn wagon to come down this road anyway. at one time this had been a major thorough-fare, but now it was no more than just an overgrown pathway. it didn't connect anywhere, not with a road or anything. the sounds grew louder. he looked at his grandmother's back, but she continued to walk at her brisk pace, seeming to notice nothing. she had been relatively quiet this night. he didn't like to disturb her when she was in one of her moods. finally, as they reached the last turn in the path, the sound, which had grown louder by this time, came to a sudden halt.

-move over herman. let the wagon pass.

-ma'am?

herman looked again, but all he could see was the enveloping darkness in front of him and the shadows that his grandmother and he cast upon the road from the moon rising behind them.

-ma'am?

he repeated again, afraid that he had heard correctly.

-didn't you hear me, boy? move out the way so the wagon can pass.

herman looked, but could see nothing.

-what wagon? grandma? i don't see anything.

-that's cause you don't know how to look. besides you don't have to see anything, just move.

the boy peered into the approaching night, beginning to think for the first time that the things he had heard about his grandmother's strangeness and her spirit were true.

-chile, just come on over here and stand next to me.

he was still standing in the middle of the road. gently she grabbed his arm and pulled him off to the shoulder. as she did he could hear the creaking of the wheels slowly begin again. the clump, clump, clumping of a mule passed so close he could feel the breath of the mule hot on his face. as the sounds passed he noticed his grandmother slightly nod her head. eyes down, into the nothingness of the night she gave a small smile and a quiet

-how do.

just as he was beginning to think that she was losing her mind he noticed the set of tracks in the dust of the road. a perfectly matched set of wagon wheel tracks, like those he had seen many many times before, along with the hoof prints of a mule. except this time he had seen no wagon. he stared at the receding tracks, following them with his eyes, unbelievingly. as he watched they grew in the direction of the fading sound, keeping pace with the creaking which moved ever so slowly away and eventually out of earshot.

he looked at his grandmother. wonder, curiosity and uncertainty was written all across his face, but she took no notice. she had just about closed the remaining distance to the fence which sectioned off her yard from the surrounding woods. he turned and moved hesitantly into a broken run in his effort to catch up to her. he turned back occasionally to look over his shoulder as the sounds of the wagon receded. when he reached his grandmother, he said gently

-i don't understand.

she turned to look at the bewildered boy in front of her.

-ain't nothing to understand.

standing there in his patched overalls in the darkening night
in the red dust of the georgia road with that look on his face
she remembered her virgil.

the moon had finally risen, breaking through the two little
clouds which had held back his brilliance. upon making his
appearance the wooded night was lit up by the splendor of
his presence.

-what did you see?

the boy looked at the wrinkled face of his grandmother,
realizing for the first time what a beauty she was and must
have been. it was as if the moonlight had brought out a
beauty recessed for ages. it was as if he were really seeing her
for the first time.

-i don't know. what happened?

-what did you see? is more the point.

it was hard for him to form the words because he wasn't exactly sure of what it was he had just witnessed.

-well, speak up boy. what did you see?

he shook his head. what had he seen? just some tracks that had not been there and then they were.

- you must always look. not just with your eyes here,

she said, pointing to his head,

-but with the eyes of your soul.

-but there were tracks, i saw them.
wagon tracks and the sound of a mule.
it was so close i could feel the heat of its breath...

his grandmother looked at him, pleased, in spite of herself.

-they just some of them that have gone on ahead,
to prepare a way,

she said so softly under her breath that the boy could barely hear it. she said nothing else as she walked into the front door of her cabin. she returned with a piece of rock candy for him.

-be careful with your gift.

he thought at the time that she had meant his candy. she held out her leathery chin. he kissed her before turning to start the journey home. he wasn't scared, exactly, but he had a lot to think about.

sucking on the road candy as he passed the tracks, he stopped to examine them more closely. he stooped to touch them, they were real. it was then he ran all the way home.

★ ★ ★

blue mountains

old man's sport
for mustapha and jihad

daddy franklin could begin to see the stretch toward ninety-eight. when people would talk about his reaching the century mark he would smile but say nothing. he knew he would never see a hundred.

whenever asked the secret of his longevity his only answer was always,

-god don't want me, devil won't have me,

then he would laugh, his toothless gums sparkling in the daylight. he had heard the argument all his life. when he was younger it had been just a murmur. as he had gotten older it had slowly become louder and louder. finally he had been able to discern the separate voices and then finally the gist of the argument. he would smile,

-you only walk up this hill so far and no more.

those who knew him well suspected it was the turtle soup.

-it's old man's sport,

he would say.

-turtles and me go along about at the same speed.
a goodmatch.

daddy had a huge appetite and was always at breakfast. daddy truly loved to eat, especially in preparation to do battle with the turtles. breakfast was always a huge affair. cold or hot cereal, biscuits, fresh homemade hot apple sauce, pancakes, bacon, sausage, scrambled eggs, country ham, last night's chicken or roast, fresh fried fish, grits, home fried potatoes, the ever present cucumber and tomato in vinegar and whatever else big mama had a taste for. there would be daddy, the first one at the table, negotiating the fried corn with no teeth. daddy was able to eat anything. he hadn't had a tooth in his head in over fifty years. those weathered gums would prove a match for any set of dentures.

it was always at or right after breakfast that daddy terrorized the little children with offers of vanilla milk from his withered right nipple or chocolate from the withered left that peeked out from behind little wisps of silver white hairs which stood standing straight out from his ancient chest. great-grandsons would scream and scatter in an attempt to escape the forced feeding. daddy would stand and laugh and laugh and laugh. big mama would just shake her head.

his great-grandsons would watch his figure fading slowly up over the hill, growing smaller in the early morning light, leaning on his walking stick, empty canvas bag thrown over his shoulder. they would play all day, with one eye on the hill, waiting for him to return home, sometimes until dusk.

daddy enjoyed the battle. the battle with the turtles was a metaphysical event. they grew to know each other, he and the turtles, to understand the ways of one another. as he grew older they were evenly matched. each could prove a danger to the other.

the turtles could hear him coming and he could smell them. daddy would follow their traces through the valley between the blue mountains, an ancient valley, a swamp-like wilderness with overgrown woods reminiscent of prehistoric underbrush. he and the turtles moved at about the same speed. the turtles moved along as one slow herd. if daddy was too slow and allowed a leg to be caught between the ancient reptilian jaws it could prove fatal. he had seen what could be done to tree limbs he had used as walking sticks. it was here in the habitation of the turtles that battles raged. after years of continued conflict, the adversaries had grown to respect and even love one another.

there had developed a particular friendship with one large male whom daddy named buster. buster was the undisputed leader of the turtle tribe and had guided his clan to a successful flourishing in this swamp for more than fifty years. daddy had been beaten, outsmarted, outflanked and outmaneuvered on more than a few occasions. they had battled some nearly forty years ago when daddy had first set foot into the primordial forest. in the course of forty years they found in each other not only worthy opponents but a lasting friendship. this friendship with buster which outlived all of his others, had been solidified when finally they understood that they were able to communicate, able to read each other's thoughts. there had been a time last year when, after not seeing buster for nearly five years, he had come upon him, waiting. he hadn't even retreated into his shell. he seemed as happy to see daddy as daddy was to see him. they had sat there, facing one another, like old friends visiting until near dark. daddy had been the first to turn and head for home.

by then daddy had more than a hunter's interest in turtles or more precisely, turtle soup.

-mable, hey you mable!

-what is it daddy?

-mable, hey you mable!

-comin' daddy, what is it?

-mable, hey you mable!

-yeah daddy? what you want?

-mable, hey you mable, girl cook me up this turtle i done caught chere. gots my mouth worked up for some turtle soup, do lord. gots my mouth a fixed up to tasting some of your turtle soup.

-you want turtle soup now, papa?
you know what time it is?
you know how long it gonna take to cook?

-mable, hey you mable, get that water boiling now,
'cause you know i wants turtle soup tonight.
i gots plans for evening.

-plans? what sort of plans?

-none of your never mind what sort of plans,
just cook up this chere turtle. whew, so heavy,
i couldn't even bring back the shell.
was a time...

-you better leave them big heavy shells
just where they is, old as you are.

-woman, don't you be all the time worrying over me,
look to your own self.
i ain't no chile to be coddled to.

-everybody can see that daddy, you old coon.

the great-grandsons would clear the kitchen and retreat to
the doorways before he could open up the canvas sack
oozing the brownish green turtle blood. one of the great-
grandsons would be dispatched to get some newspaper, one
to get some water from the well, one for daddy's hunting
knife and another for the big black cooking pan from under

the oven. the great-grandsons would escape into the evening
of fireflies and leave the postmortem to daddy and big mama.

-can't understand why you gotta have turtle soup tonight.
ain't gonna be ready no time soon.

-mable, hey you mable, stop all that fussin', you hear?
just fix me my soup.

-i am daddy.

mable, his daughter, mother of thirteen, eleven living, big
mama to all the nearly forty some odd grandchildren, would
grumble and fuss some. she would complain about the late-
ness of the hour or the trouble and the mess, but she was a
good daughter. she loved and always obeyed her father and
he in turn loved and cherished her.

-i have places to go.

-i can't hurry it up anymore than i can, daddy.
it's gotta cook. lessin' you want it raw?
you know that turtle wild as it wanna be,
so you just ought ta let it cook slow.

daddy franklin knew he would be busy until the early hours
of the morning and he was anxious for the night to begin.
he would need all his strength. it was not easy to totally
satisfy a woman with needs like miss prime and he had every
intention of doing so. he had been a widower at a young

age. it didn't take long for him to realize how many widow women there were around in need. didn't seem to make too much sense in marrying again, considering he had curtailed his goings on as age had determined and demanded. he was down to only one night a week, saturday night. oh how he did live for blessed saturday night and the lips of sweet miss prime. why not?

-he had a young dark honey,

he would confide to his great-grandsons,

-and she had a powerful need.

then he would wink, as he sat down to finish two full bowls of piping hot turtle soup.

-keep you going through the night,

he would say between mouthfuls, winking down at the soup.

miss prime wouldn't be forty-seven until the beginning of the next year. shit...she still had her looks. miss prime had a great smile. in fact it had been her smile that had first attracted him. they had been in line at the supermarket when he had noticed her polygrip. instant love. his reply to questions concerning his continued virility and love making into his nineties was always the same,

-one doesn't live until your woman loses her teeth.

he would smile his toothless grin.

> -give me a woman who puts her teeth in a jar every night.
> i got something for her!

he would laugh lewdly,

> -she'll wake up in paradise each and every morning.
> when i see those teeth sitting up in that cup,
> boy i can feel something else sitting up, my passion rising.

> -daddy, leave them children alone.
> they don't need to hear all that.

> -mable, hey you mable, go on now,
> this chere ain't none of your business no how.
> this chere is men's talk.

his great-grandsons would feel proud and important, they would sit up listening more intently, more like men.

the great-grandsons would stand around the table and watch daddy eat the turtle soup. they were mesmerized with horror. they would retreat into doorways to assure the turtle soup didn't come anywhere near them. they were repulsed by the reptile meat floating in its greenish brown broth. daddy would offer some of it to each of his great-grandsons ceremonially. he would howl in laughter as they each turned up their noses, refused it and ran.

after supper he would bathe in the big round tub in the kitchen. one of his great-grandsons would soap his back while another would pour the water to rinse. he would dress in his best summer suit, dress shoes and straw hat or in colder months his gray-blue pinstripe suit, dress boots and dark hat cocked to the side; bow tie, handkerchief, suspenders and mahogany walking stick.

        -looking right sharp there, mr. franklin,

big mama would admire as he strolled toward the steps of the front porch. the cab driver would open the door for him.

      -mable, hey you mable, don't wait up for me you hear?

he would say from the window before the cab rolled off down the hill.

      -yes, daddy. i won't latch the screen door.
       i'll leave the porch light on.

they would watch the dust rise behind the cab as it disappeared down the hill. big mama would awaken many a morning to turn the porch light off herself, the sun having risen with no sign of benjamin franklin in sight. usually it was after dawn when she would hear his staggering steps trying to negotiate the front porch. the cab driver would be holding him up, trying to shove money daddy had taken out back into daddy's wallet, relieved that big mama had come out so that it all could be left in her hands. she would put her arms around his chest and struggle to make it upstairs to his bed. then of course there was daddy singing, loud enough to wake the dead. great-grandsons would slowly appear sleepily to witness the return of the conquering hero. daddy would be in great spirits, his clothes every which way, suspenders on backwards, sometimes his pants.

                    -honestly, daddy!

                    -what woman?

he would ask,

                    -what? respect your elders,

he would admonish before he would break into song.

        -really and at your age. you ought to know better.

                    -i was better,

he would laugh heartily,

                    -and what's age got to do with it?
                    everything still works.
                    miss prime can attest to that.
                       i gotta witness,

he would laugh,

                    -i gotta witness!

he would confide to his great-grandsons that he would fill
them in on all the sticky details as soon as this woman would
let him alone.

-y'all go on and get back in the bed.

-just not as often as i would like,

he would continue,

-but it worked tonight, do jesus! didn't miss a stroke.
lover man. called me her special lover man.
mable, hey you mable, you hear that?

-i don't wanna be hearing all that now papa.
just go on to bed.
you ought to be getting up and going to church
with me, lover man,

big mama would admonish, halfheartedly. she tried to sup-
press the laughter growing inside herself as she pulled off his
shoes and put daddy to bed.

-woman, i don't need to go to church!
i just got back from praying.
lord, i done found me religion, and her name is <u>miss prime</u>!
and don't be waking me up this morning none.
this morning i'm sleeping in late.

he would sing again as he drifted off to sleep.

-if he ain't saved my soul by now, he don't want it,
he would mumble as he fell off to sleep, the sound of the
eternal argument running through his head.

-never too late...

she would begin. he would be snoring before she reached
the steps.

----

daddy would spend the remainder of his week in anticipa-
tion of his saturday night pursuits. his daily activities consisted of sitting on the porch watching the tracks the sun had
made, watching the fruit trees ripen or the rains. he admit-
ted watching the endless trains traveling distances at full
throttle across his field of vision, wishing upon them,
sending his magic across the land as he had done for nearly
a century.

without a doubt his driving weekday passion was the pity-
pat games he would lure his great-grandsons into, as well as
any unsuspecting victim who happened his way. he was a
vicious pity-pat player. sitting, looking over his cards,
studying the cards as they hit the table, studying the
opposing players, chewing tobacco, spitting. he was crafty. if
you were to have a chance at beating him you had to match
his skill and wit. he would cheat and tell lewd jokes. cheat
without hesitation, if you didn't watch. hell, he would cheat
even if you did and he enjoyed it. cheating was as much fun
as playing. he enjoyed cheating and not getting caught. he
enjoyed cheating when he did get caught. he enjoyed
cheating and winning as he did everything else in life, fully,
completely.

playing cards with his great-grandsons, who were his true joy, his crowning glory, gave him great pleasure. the idea of great-grandsons pleased him. he taught them the important lessons of life, lessons that would stay with them the rest of their lives, lessons they would be richer for knowing. this was his legacy to them. this was their inheritance. it was here that he imparted the magic he had accumulated over a lifetime. he taught them the importance and the unimportance of the game, the sanctity of laughter, the enjoyment of one another and the value of the moment, this, any, every moment. his love, his joy was infectious and his lineage grew strong, nurtured by the twinkling in his eyes. they were the flowering of the tree, he was its root.

there was not a soul who had met daddy franklin who didn't love him. his was a great responsibility, to love and to be loved for ninety-seven years.

the image of daddy and his great-grandsons around him would remain. it had been this way for almost twenty years since he had gone to live with his daughter after her husband died. they had been, daughter and father, good company for each other. in all the time they had lived together, had argued, fought and loved one another, they had come to understand and know each other's ways. each of them had been the comfort the other needed. together they had fought off time, but even still the argument was drawing to a close. daddy knew he would never see a hundred.

finally, heaven and hell came to a compromise. suddenly, one day, the haggling came to an end, there was only silence.

daddy sat up and took notice. it was a perfectly still tuesday morning in february. it was clear but cold. his daughter heard him call her from the front room. she ran from the kitchen. she ran as she hadn't since she had been a little girl, the wet dishtowel still in her hands. she recognized death, it was in the tone of his voice and she knew immediately.

-daddy?

he was stricken, pale, on the couch. he was holding his stomach, not quite able to catch his breath. he held out his hand to his only child and squeezed her arm tightly. he asked her for a glass of water so she should not witness his leaving. when she returned he was gone. as she bent over the quiet prostrate figure of her father the glass quietly slipped from her hand. she checked for breathing, but she knew. he was gone. he had left quietly, quickly, without fanfare or bother.

this would be the last time they would get to spend alone together. she sat in the chair across from him and rocked. she looked up at the pictures of her children and grandchildren, his grandchildren and great-grandchildren, which hung over the couch where her daddy lay, the debate between god and the devil finally settled. sitting there she reconstructed for herself the chronology of his life. she had time to remember everything about him. time to give thanks for the blessing his life had been and the blessings his life had given. time to be comforted that she had been there when he left. time to be thankful that she had had this time to say goodbye. time to adjust to the weight of the family that had slipped so silently onto her shoulders, they were hers now.

there had been no one to hold big mama when she had to say goodbye to daddy. she never did cry. there was no reason.

by the time her granddaughter found them, her goodbyes were complete. she wouldn't let any of them cry, not even at the the funeral.

-hush,

she would say when any of them would begin.

-he lived a good and long life, to a ripe old age.
he had a full and rewarding time.
he lived fully the life he was given.
he loved and was loved.
he enjoyed life and that is all any of us can hope to do.
don't dishonor him with your tears.

only one of his great-grandsons wondered about the turtles. it was he who had seen the huge turtle on the day of the funeral. right before they left the house.

the turtle had come about halfway down the hill from the direction daddy took on those saturday mornings. he stood to pay respect for a part of the day.

when the boy looked he was gone.

★ ★ ★

sandwich

for walter and mable

the sun at the quarry was relentless. the men glistened in the heat
of the noon day sun. the only sound was the whistle of picks
in air hitting rock which gave itself grudgingly, reluctantly.
returning rhythmically, the sound of the picks hitting ungiving
rock cast a hypnotic spell over the men. it was a meditation. each
man lost in his rhythm yet connected firmly to the sound of the
whole and his place within its framework. bronze skin shim-
mered in the heat, rolling across the expanse of the granite in
waves.

the whistle sounded. men returned from the distances to which
they had traveled. slowly the men broke, each searching for
refuge, attempting to find or create shade and take in water. no
one spoke, the heat was loud enough. slowly, after exhausting
methods to escape the sun, they settled down to the comforts
found in crumpled and oil soaked brown bags. those meager
provisions of sustenance, packed with the love and promise of
women whose intention was sustaining the strength of their
menfolk until they returned to their tables at supper.

walter lewis wiped the sweat from his brow with the white
handkerchief he found every morning next to the clean pair of

overalls and white tee shirt that were laid out so carefully on the chair, the brown bag sitting on the table near the back door. vainly he tried to keep back the flowing perspiration from his balding head. finally he settled for dipping the handkerchief into some water, wringing it out and putting it on his head.

after convincing himself that he had achieved some modicum of relief, he reached for his lunch. he anticipated the small feast his wife mable had prepared. there were two things he could say about mable, she could fix a good meal and she could make love. he still remembered the first day he saw her. he had loved her then, as a girl of sixteen and had not stopped loving her for one moment since. sometimes as the children ran across the yard, he would catch sight of her and watching her he would fall in love all over again. there had been births, so many births, each as miraculous as the ones before. they had known only the solitude of peace until leroy, their eldest, had been hit over the head and lain in the snow to die. he had thought he might lose mable as well when they had to put their child in the ground. she wouldn't leave the grave for days, grieving that she couldn't leave him out there alone. it was the birth of another child which did much to restore her spirit.

there was indeed a reason why the lights went out at eight every night, a reason why they were expecting the birth of the ninth of their eventual thirteen children. mable grey lee bertha fannie anne lou ella may franklin lewis could cook and she could fuck! lord a'mercy. her mother had named her mable and the name and order of each of her friends who had come to visit during her time of confinement. she had loved her only daughter dearly and her legacy was she taught her how to prepare food and how to love. her daughter had learned well.

walter lewis reached in the bag, discovering the three deviled eggs wrapped neatly in wax paper, the triangular wrappings that held two of mable's delicious half moon apple pies and what appeared to be a tremendous sandwich. his mouth began to water as he thought of the virginia ham he had just finished hickory smoking from one of the winter hogs he had fattened up all spring. the anticipated saltiness from the ham would help to retain needed water for this afternoon's work. he caught the eyes of crawford staring as he furtively tried to wipe his greasy mouth.

at first walter lewis noticed nothing out of the ordinary. the sandwich was overflowing with the fillings mable had added to complement the choice pieces she had cut off this morning. as he chewed the first bite he noticed the problem. the second bite convinced him. he confirmed it when he opened the sandwich to find it had everything except the ham. his first thought was how surprised mable would be when she found out she had left out the ham in the ham sandwich!

he brought the opened sandwich to his nose. there was the unmistakable lingering smell of fresh cut hickory smoked virginia ham. he looked at the sandwich curiously. it was when he brought the sandwich up to his nose a second time that his eye caught crawford staring at him. licking his lips, crawford looked away as soon as he saw walter lewis' eyes on him.

walter lewis was a big man. when he stood his full six foot three, his two hundred and twenty pound frame was impressive. he slowly strode across the open field toward crawford who looked more and more apprehensive as he approached.

-uh, how do lewis?

silence. walter lewis said nothing. he walked over to crawford and literally pulled him to his feet.

-what you doin' that for lewis?
is you done gone and lost your mind?
you ain't got no cause to be treatin' me this way.

walter lewis paid him no mind.

-what's got into you lewis?

-i smell ham off you crawford,
fresh cut hickory smoked virginia ham.

there was no denial. walter lewis grabbed crawford around the neck with one of his powerful hands and forced the middle finger down his throat until he returned to him what was his. the freshly chewed ham hadn't even gotten a chance to be digested. walter lewis drew back his strong pick welding hand and deposited it with all his force on the jaw of crawford. you could hear the break on contact.

they had just finished filling the new quarry with water. walter lewis dragged crawford to its edge.

-if you ever mess with anything that belongs to me or
my family again, as sure as i am standing here,
i will beat you to within an inch of your life.

then he unceremoniously threw him in and walked away.
everyone knew how scared crawford was of the water. he was
so scared of drowning they said he didn't bathe. walter lewis
did not look back. if john dokes hadn't come to his rescue,
there was little doubt that crawford would have drowned on
that day.

----

the children would wait on papa -- every evening. as the
shadows would begin to grow long they would sit or stand
near the big oak tree in the middle of the yard so they could
catch the first glimpse of his figure in the settling dusk. then
they would begin the race down the hill to see who would
reach him first.

walter lewis would stop and watch his children. he would wait
to touch or hug each child, tired as he was. then he would
pick up the youngest, put her on his shoulder and start the
walk up the hill. he would reach into his pocket to pull out
the assortment of peppermint balls or other hard candies he
had stopped on franklin hill to buy for their searching hands.

-mable

he would call, as he reached the top of the hill,

-get these children off me.
i done worked hard all day in the white man's sun.
when do we eat, miss mable?
today i'm as hungry as a bear.
i done worked a colored man's day and i'm so tired i'm
about to drop.

-you children, get in here.
you mary, turn that chicken, you annie, set the table,
you mable, cut up some cucumber and tomato,
you mason, bring in some cold water from the well,
you earl, feed them chickens, you stewart,
pick me some green apples--i feel like some hot apple sauce,
you nina, put the food on the table and you fannie, ah...
just bring in the drinking glasses and place them on the
table.

everyone had a real job except fannie, who claimed to be so
sickly she couldn't do anything. she was papa's favorite or so
she believed. the truth was walter lewis loved each of his children, each in a special way.

big mama shouted orders like a drill sergeant, the kitchen
literally blazing with activity. the cadence of

-ma'am, yes ma'am
was repeated until the table was full. finally everyone was
washed, seated and prayed over. walter lewis looked over his
growing clan and was well pleased.

everyone sat up as papa cleared his throat.

-that was a fine lunch you fixed me today mable.
'course i could'a done with a little meat.

-what you talkin' 'bout walter lewis?
i cut you some fine slices of that first summer ham.

he laughed at the look of consternation on her face.

-oh, i didn't say you didn't cut it,
i said i didn't get any of it.
there was a rather large field mouse tried to get away
with it, but i think he won't be eating anythin'
for a little while, at least nothin'
that's not through a straw.

then he told them the story of his day.

they laughed about that thing for weeks and those weeks
turned into years. mable got up early that next day and made
sure she fixed walter lewis a particularly nice lunch, with two
sandwiches and an especially large piece of apple cobbler.
walter lewis ate a particularly good lunch every day from that
day until the day he died.

★ ★ ★

cherry

for earl, mason, stuart and billy

the lewis boys stood on the back porch and watched as cherry slowly made her way over the apex of the hill and disappeared from sight into the morning sunrise.

every morning cherry ambled over the hill, in no apparent hurry. she found the uphill trip home easier, returning to the stable over at the vaughns, relieved as she was of her sacred load. the red dust from the clay road lifted softly in the morning air. as she walked, her tail traveled listlessly from side to side in response to the horsefly who had chosen to keep her company on this her daily vigil.

vaughn had admired the red cow lewis owned for years. every few seasons he had tried to buy the cow but lewis would not hear of it.

                    -when the time's right

was all lewis would say.

one spring before the birth of a seventh daughter and the building of the new well, lewis sold cherry to vaughn.

the lewis boys looked down at the full bucket and a half of milk and cream that cherry just delivered into their familiar hands as she had and would each and every morning of her lactating life. milking at the lewis farm was at four-thirty and despite the three quarters of a mile cherry now had to travel. she was never late.

vaughn, who milked at six, could never figure out why the red cow he had purchased from lewis was always dry.

and lewis never told him why.

★ ★ ★

abominable snowman
for james barkley jr.

-did you hear about the lynching?

the question still echoed in his mind minutes after he had hung
up from talking to his friend.

-what lynching? what are you talking about?

-some brother in ohio, about sixty miles
from the aryan nation headquarters.

-lynched?

he still couldn't quite comprehend the meaning.

-lynched! tied from a tree, hands tied behind his back,
swinging, found hanging in the breeze!

-when?

-this morning.

-are you serious?

-as cancer.

he couldn't believe it and then he could. after all what was the difference? eleanor bumpers had been a lynching. michael stewart had been a lynching. yusef hawkins had been a lynching. there weren't any bodies hanging from trees, but what had been the difference? they were just as surely dead. howard beach, that cannibal in milwaukee, the sister at st. john's, the list was endless. what the fuck was going on? but this, this was somehow different. with this there was the visual picture.

-what fucking year is this?

they both said at the same time.

-it's getting dangerous,

laughed james, referring to the number of times that they had said the same things at the same time recently.

-strange fruit,

they both said together.

-that's it, it's too much. i'm outta here,

howled james.

-later.

he laughed, knowing that he would probably talk to james at

least five more times before the day was out. but yo! this was no joke. motherfuckers were lynching folks.

-did you hear about the lynching?

it rumbled around inside his head, as flashes of memory tugged at him, like photographs in a picture album, old, black and white, some a little wrinkled, worn, yellowing on the back and just around the edges. he was sitting on his grandmother's porch with his great-grandfather, listening to his cousins asking for money to go to the movies.

-y'all take little dean along too.

he sat up at the mention of his name. the movies? sure, why not? all his cousins were older than he, the ones there. tommy, belinda, cc, robert.

belinda grabbed his hand, promised his mother to take care of him and they were off, up the rocky red dirt path, past geneiva and babe brother's house, through the shortcut in the woods near the old hog pens, through the blackberry fields and finally to the road, up past the church at cedar green toward franklin hill and town. the cousins argued as to whether they should take the bus or walk and save the extra money for candy. it was hot and the bus pulled up.

belinda gave dean the money for the bus and let go of his hand as he climbed on first. he dropped the money in and made his way to the first seat that faced front and climbed in next to the window.

-what you doing boy?

whispered belinda, as she grabbed his hand and jerked him toward the back.

-what's wrong?

he cried, for he had sat where he always did when he rode the bus at home.

-you ain't in new york now. we got to sit in the back.

-why?

he asked innocently.

-white people sit in the front,
colored people sit in the back, here.

he didn't ask any more questions or even comment on it. it seemed an equitable enough arrangement to his five-year old mind, something for everyone. besides, this was the first time he had ridden in the back.

but it was at the movies that his coming of age occurred. *the abominable snowman* was playing. they had bought candy and soda at the store down franklin hill when they had gotten off the bus. they went into the movies, upstairs and down to the very front of the balcony. during the entire movie he was sure he was going to fall off the edge so he sat very still and watched in amazement the death defying antics of his cousins as they hung over the railing. they bounced up and down, yelled and screamed as the monster thawed and came back to life.

he whispered to his cousin belinda that he wanted some popcorn and that he wanted to sit downstairs. he was frightened by the swaying of the balcony and he wanted to sit downstairs like he always did with his aunt me me when she would take him to the movies at home.

-we can't buy anything from the candy stand downstairs, that's only for white people. we can't sit downstairs neither.

-well, where is the candy stand for us?

-there isn't any and there ain't no bathroom.

he didn't say anymore.

when he got home, his father asked him how he liked the movies. he told him the movie had been good, but that he liked the movies at home much better. he then proceeded to tell him about his day. his father was furious. his mother had allowed him to go without his permission.

-don't you ever worry again. i'll drive you anyplace you have to go. i'll buy you all the popcorn and candy you want.

ain't no son of mine gonna sit in the back of no bus!

in this way, his father tried to protect him from the beckoning hand of racism but the damage had been done.

★ ★ ★

redhook

crossing the river
for fannie

the little boy awoke early. he lay in bed and listened to the stillness of the morning. there was only the muffled sound of last night's rain, the occasional splash of car wheels hitting puddles. there was a laziness in the change from night to day as if the night was reticent in giving up his darkness and the day not anxious to dress in her light. the little boy rose and quietly turned on the television to watch cartoons until it was time to eat, wash and dress for church.

----

the right reverend and mrs. cato lived on the second floor of the small storefront church on the edge of the neighborhood that held the red brick housing project development. from her bedroom window mrs. cato could look out and by turning her head to the left could see a corner of the large shipping yard. today, as it was sunday, there was little activity on the docks.

she listened to the steady breathing of the reverend as she pulled the worn sides of the bathrobe across her chest. she had been standing at the window since the first streaks of daylight and felt a slight chill. instinctively, she crossed her arms over her stomach and the growing life within. mothering had already begun.

she turned to look over the dark figure entwined amongst the covers. she could make out the steady slow pattern of breathing as the sheets softly rose and fell to the intake and release of air. he began to stir. he was still completing the journey back from sleep. the shore of waking could be seen in the distance, yet consciousness had not yet been achieved. she realized that this feeling of secret sharing she felt with the child would soon be ending. she would tell him today.

she knew what pressure he had been under. she knew the deacon board would be there today. she knew what it meant to their future. this was not their first placement. they had yet to stay any one place for more than two years. it was not the reverend's fault. congregations were unpredictable, as were their funds. in fact, the reverend had started working a couple of days at the docks to supplement the meager collection plates. she didn't want to add more pressure to his shoulders.

she laid back down on the bed as the reverend opened his eyes, pulling himself slowly back into this reality. he was surprised by the amorous touches he awakened to and their sudden cessation as he watched his wife run to the bathroom. she had barely reached the toilet before she began retching her dry guts out.

----

the little boy walked in the shadow of his mother. he slowly brought up the rear, reluctantly. she strode determinedly,

not even looking behind her. she reached out her hand at
the corner. he turned to look longingly at the monkey-bars
in the center of the playground and the set of painted concrete barrels. his thoughts were on the ring-o-levio game
that would be played there in a couple of hours. he listened
as his mother explained where he was to meet her at the end
of sunday school. as she did each sunday, she would go
home, dress and change. she would be waiting for him
downstairs, at the bottom of the steps, near the back
entrance. she had to sing today, which meant she would walk
in with the rest of the choir. he would have to sit through
service alone.

----

sunday school class had been taken over by sister jones. mrs.
cato had not felt well. as the congregation arrived for the
eleven-thirty service, the small storefront church slowly filled
up. as mrs. cato made her way to her seat at the upright
piano, a few sisters looked quizzically at her and spoke in
hushed tones among themselves. the rustle of the choir
gathering in place in the stairwell at the rear of the church
which led to the parsonage above signaled readiness for
service.

the little boy sat in the second row, on the aisle, as he had
been instructed. as the church filled, he felt somewhat isolated. among the rows of parishioners he felt small. he was
cut off from sight of the seat where his mother would sit
upright, among the altos, dressed in her maroon robe with

gold collar and sleeves. suddenly a pathway of sight cleared as seats were changed. a little girl, with three meticulously parted braids and nine pink and yellow barrettes swinging gently past her shoulders was now in the seat directly in front of him. she being smaller, he now had the entire pulpit in his sight line.

the opening strains of the upright piano signaled the rising of the congregation and the beginning of the processional. the choir sang

> *-we are climbing jacob's ladder,*

as they stepped out in unison.

> *-we are climbing jacob's ladder,*

the congregation turned.

> *-we are climbing jacob's ladder,*
> *-soldiers of the fort.*

> *-every round goes higher and higher*

the choir clapped.

> *-every round goes higher and higher,*

the boy clapped too; it was one of his favorites.

-every round goes higher and higher,
-soldiers of the fort.

the song continued, step by step, round by round, until the entire choir, ushers, deacons and elders followed by the right reverend cato climbed the steps to the pulpit and moved into place. this was the most exciting time for the little boy. he liked pageantry. by the time the opening hymn and prayer were over, he returned to himself. from here it would be a long haul.

----

the bible selection for the day was being read and discussed. the boy began to drift, remembering yesterday's ring-o-levio game.

----

the boy is brought back into the small storefront church as the choir stands to sing.

-upon a mountain far away i wandered sad and 'lone
-then jesus came and found me there and i became his own
-his loving arms enfolded me close to his bleeding side
-now i am his and he is mine
-praise god i'm satisfied.

the boy looked around and realized that it had become time. young as he was he had learned to recognize the time of spirit.

-i'm satisfied,
-satisfied with jesus
-satisfied
-satisfied with jesus
-he said,
-he said he'd be my comfort
-he said,
-he said he'd be my guide
-i looked at my hands, my hands looked new
-i looked at my feet and they did too
-and ever since that wonderful day, my soul's been
-satisfied.

–have you crossed the river?
have you seen the shore on the other side?

and with this the right reverend cato began the time of
spirit. he had a special thanks today. his wife had told him
of their expectation. he was fired up and as the boatman for
the lord planned to bring a number of worshippers across
today.

this was the time that the boy looked forward to the least.
this was a time of danger, especially for an unprotected child.
it wasn't the talking in tongues, though he had to admit after
so many years of listening that there was a spirit language
being spoken. he just didn't know what it was that was being
said. no the real danger was if someone near you received
the visitation of the holy ghost and in that ecstasy fell on you
or knocked you across the room. that and the vacancy

within the eyes the visited experienced sent true terror through him. along with the fact that what scared him the most was that the spirit took whom it pleased. it was at this time of spirit that he prayed fervently each week. today was no exception. he prayed that the spirit would come soon, because even at this young age he knew they would not be released until the spirit had touched someone and he prayed that it wouldn't be him. he could think of nothing more frightening than having yourself possessed by a ghost, even if it was holy and to find yourself thrown around the floor, shaking, eyes rolling back, talking in tongues. but he knew there would be no closing benediction until there had been a talking in tongues, a crossing over. even if it took all day, it was why they had come, it was why they were here.

it had been the ability of the right reverend cato to usher members of the congregation across the river of tongues that had allowed the right reverend to be hired, for he knew the way across the waters to the land of canaan. he knew how to bring them to the place where the waters met the land. the place where spirit would come to visit.

the little boy's attention was drawn for some reason to the three braided girl in front of him. he was the only one to notice the shiver that ran through her. he watched as she touched the pant leg of the brown suit which sat next to her. he watched the hat float downward as the brown suit suddenly went stiff, throwing himself backwards, knocking over his chair and the one next to him and with it sending the fat blue and white dress to the floor. it was her mother next who suddenly started to jump up and down as she touched the three braided girl, shaking, her eyes

rolled back in her head as she viewed first hand the land of
canaan from within, blessing the congregation in tongue. the
three braided girl jumped up and down in glee as she imi-
tated the activity around her. anyone who reached for her
became enraptured.

those around them called

-praise the lord.

they tried to fan, cover, hold and give them room as more
and more people in the wake of the three braided girl's
activity fell, succumbed to the power of the spirit.

for the first time sister cato felt the baby inside her move.

the little boy watched the trail of havoc which followed the
three braided girl as she hopped around, sending another and
another of the parishioners to the land across the river on the
other side.

the congregation talked for hours in tongues. the right
revered cato would be given an open-ended contract after
this day. more and more people found themselves bound for
canaan before the three braided girl found herself a seat
among the many tongues and fell asleep.

the little boy watched and kept clear of her. he remembered
and silently thanked her, for he knew that soon it would be
time to go home. he was too exhausted for the ring-o-levio
game today. he didn't understand and never would. he also
was very sure never to touch or sit near the girl with the
three braids ever again.

★ ★ ★

warrior seed
for nina

the aunt peered from behind the six story window. her attention had been diverted from the conversation occurring behind
her. she looked across the living room adoringly at her husband
earnestly engaged in conversation with her brother-in-law.
unaware, her sister continued her monologue. she did not notice
the split attention the aunt was giving her.

from the window of the apartment the aunt could see as far away
as the statue of liberty standing in the harbor that partially surrounded the red brick project development. she could see the
fields where baseball and football were played. behind them she
could see the pool, crowded in the summer heat with the children of the large housing complex. she could view the line of
stores where children spent their little change on candies and
other non-food items. but what grabbed her attention was
much closer to home.

her eyes blazed. anyone who knew the woman knew you did
not want to be the object of her ire. she had always had a temper. always had an unbreakable spirit, a fire. she took shit from
no one. make no mistake, she would fight and kick ass or two
as was necessary. this time her attention was drawn to the crowd

of children in the rectangular piece of concrete that served as the playground for the immediate set of buildings. the nephew could feel the heat of her stare from that distance without having to look up. the aunt met him at the door of 6b.

-boy, what happened out there?

-i lost the fight.

-you got your ass kicked is more like it.
why you let that boy beat you like that?

-let him beat me? is that what you think
happened out there?

the nephew thought to himself. he said simply,

-i fought him as good as i could.

-and he kicked your ass.

the aunt reached for a cigarette. the nephew was frustrated. he had indeed given everything that he had inside his seven-year old body. no one liked getting beat. the fact was sim-ple: justin. his best friend. had been for as long as he could remember. justin lived downstairs. in 2b. the same age. justin three months older. they had lived for the sight of one another since their mothers had first introduced them in their strollers. they had known each other as long as they had known themselves. they were as close as brothers, closer, until this last week. five consecutive fights in five days. each day justin had found another reason to argue, then pick a fight. the nephew's life had become miserable and he didn't know why.

miserable over the fact that he had lost a friendship he had so valued. miserable because justin had chosen to do this in front of the entire square. but most miserable because he couldn't beat him. it hurt his pride and it hurt! it wasn't as if he just let justin whip him. he gave it his all. it was just that at this particular moment in their mutual development, when this vestige of warrior seed had chosen to fulfill its destiny, at just this exact time, at just this entwining, justin was the bigger, the stronger, the better fighter.

-so why you let that boy beat you?

the aunt repeated. she spoke in low tones, purposely, so that their conversation in the kitchen would not be overheard by the rest of the family. the nephew was not especially interested in anyone else knowing.

-i was trying. he just better.

-how long this been going on?

-just this last week.

as the nephew thought back over the five days, the aunt read profound anguish in his face.

-never mind, it's been too damn long!
the little heifer. we'll have something for his little
black ass next time. little black devil.

the aunt's eyes blazed as she focused her mind on the fight.
the nephew felt his battle become theirs.

-well, the next time the little heifer
goes to put his black hands on you,
you pick up the biggest thing you can find and try to
knock his head off.
i tell you that's just what I would do.
i'd try to knock the head off the little demon.
try your best to kill the bastard. you just keep whipping
his ass 'til you can't raise your arm.
bet he won't bother you after that.
now how much you want to bet?
black bastard. little son of a bitch. little black devil.
one thing i can't stand is a bully. oh, i hate a bully.
makes me mad, trying to show off.
oh, i'd like to get my hands on the little black bastard.
i'd show him.

-but that ain't fighting fair.

the aunt's nostrils flared. she fought for air.

-fair! to hell with fair!
you want him to continue to kick your ass?

she had never coddled him. that was not her way. she was a terror. when her nieces and nephews saw her coming, they would
clear a path. they would be upstanding when she passed. every
one of them straightened up when she entered a room, for she did
not play. slap you in a minute. didn't care whose child you were.
tell you she'd beat your mama too, if she didn't like it.

-you think it's fair for him to beat up on you every day?
the little heifer.

the nephew wondered what a heifer was, again. he never knew,
but he knew this was not the time to ask. he thought of his
aunt. she had always been in his corner, always. she kept your
business to herself. whatever occurred between you and her
stayed between you and her and she always kept her word. if she
said she was going to do something or promised something, you
could set your watch by it. that went from a spectacular chocolate layer cake to a long promised ass whipping. she'd tear your
ass up in a minute. before you even had a chance to think about
it. when she asked a question you'd better tell her the truth. she'd
give anyone an ass whipping, whenever it was needed and it was
never questioned. kind of like the designated ass whipper. no sass,
unacceptable sigh, bucking or rolling of eyes, sucking of teeth,
talking under breath or behind back went unnoticed. all were
capital offenses. many a child had picked up his or her face from
where she had slapped it.

-got your little black ass now!!!

would be the rallying cry which sent fear through every niece and
nephew alike. in this she gave us her complete love.

-fair? listen boy, there ain't no fair!
the next time that little hellion hits you,
you better pick up a stick, a brick or whatever.
and if you don't, when you come back in here,
i'll whip your ass again, myself! now see if i don't?
i wish i could get my hands around the little heifer's throat.
and don't go crying to your mama or your daddy neither!

the nephew knew his aunt had spoken and he had heard her
promise.

-'cause your mama know i can whip her ass
and your daddy's too!

this she said louder, laughing, to include the nephew's father who
had entered the kitchen, at the same time signaling that the conversation between aunt and nephew had come to an end.

-you must be joking,

laughed the nephew's father.

-that's right, i'll lay you out too if you mess with me.

-you hear your wife?

laughed the nephew's father as the aunt's husband came in to
join them.

-you better come on in here and get your wife.

-i ain't worried. i know my honeybunch can take
care of herself.

the uncle gave his wife a hug.

-it's you i'm worried about partner,

laughed the nephew's uncle. as aunt and uncle hugged and
kissed the nephew started slowly from the room.

-don't forget what we talked about,

said the aunt pointedly. she didn't even look up. she rubbed his
head as he passed.

-what's that about?

questioned the nephew's father.

-just something between my nephew and me.

the nephew caught the look and the meaning within her glance.

----

the next day, true to form, justin started again. the rectangle was
filled with children coming back from the pool. the nephew
didn't see the group of girls gathered at the fence watching. the
nephew focused only on the silent pair of unseen eyes watching
him from the sixth story window above. the last thing the

nephew remembered was reaching for the broken piece of orange broomstick sticking out of the garbage can.

it was only when the nephew returned to his senses that he recognized the extent of the carnage that had been wrecked. havoc was rampant. justin lay crouched up against the fence, his bleeding nose and bloody face attested to the rhythm the broken piece of orange broomstick had beat out across it. in his eyes was a new look. fear, confusion and a look of respect that would remain throughout the years of their friendship, throughout justin's short life, before he fought in the war and lost the battle to drugs, walking off the building the aunt had watched from.

that night at supper only the aunt understood the exhilaration, joy, sense of self and accomplishment that was registered in the large grin the nephew carried. neither of them had spoken of the day's event and never would. only the nephew knew why he alone received the extra piece of spectacular chocolate layer cake that the aunt had baked that afternoon while standing near the open kitchen window.

★ ★ ★

ring-o-levio

for k pot, jackie, lenora, susan, little sidney, meryl, mello
and marilyn

dean's mind returned to the ring-o-levio game. he wondered where justin, gregory and gary, douglas, russell and k
pot were. he had no doubt that they were together. they
were always together, from morning to night. he would be
there with them too if he wasn't sitting here in church. they
traveled everywhere together, one unit, a crew. they were all
the same age, all born within nine months of each other.
justin was the oldest, gregory and gary were the youngest.
they all lived in buildings that faced the same courtyard.
justin lived in 2b, gregory and gary lived in 1b, dean in 6b;
all in eighty-five lorraine. russell and douglas lived in eighty-
seven and k pot lived in eighty-nine.

they were inseparable, especially when a ring-go-levio game
was being chosen up. they always managed to be on the
same side, especially in those games that included the hicks
street buildings or those from any of the surrounding court-
yards. those were the most fun. they could involve as many
as forty or fifty and could last for a full summer's day, on rare
occasions two. in those massive games it could take as long
as half an hour to choose up sides. the team that held

homebase would count to one hundred and then the game was on. anyone tagged by the homebase team and held long enough to call

-ring-o-levio one-two-three

was captured and returned to base, unless freed by one of their teammates touching homebase, calling

-free base, free base.

if captured in the initial melee, you could spend most of the game stuck on the set of rounded concrete barrels that served as home base. only the slowest, least resourceful or just plain unlucky would be caught at the beginning of the game. then the battle would be waged. it was the only way to describe the forty boys who played at the same time, alongside ten of the most confident girls.

dean remembered the events of yesterday's game that had demanded continuation today. the game had to be called for darkness and the sudden thunderstorm.

----

they had turned the corner before we were seen. crossing the field, near the public pool we spotted them first. all of them from ninety-one, the day's adversaries. we could make out that loud plaid jacket of willie's as well as the ever present red hat of ski's. we tried to move away smoothly, so as not to attract their attention. we were doing fine until we hit the avenue. there was little traffic and no parked cars. they caught sight of our movement from near the pitcher's mound of the baseball diamond. they began to run. the chase was on.

our commando unit had been out since early morning. we had managed to elude the ninety-one crew since about eleven. we had even managed to sneak in, eat lunch and return by hiding and moving in the fenced-off honeysuckle bushes that ran alongside the projects which provided the bees we caught in jars. twilight, in a row, hunting, it was our connection to nature.

but this time we had been spotted and were now forced into action. it had been a calculated risk coming across the field, from the poolside. we had gotten closer to homebase than expected. now was a good time to make our assault. homebase was filled with nearly all of our men, captured throughout the day. it was the time of day when the light helped us. the setting sun played tricks on the eyes, long shadows everywhere.

we were a fast commando unit, led by justin who was the fastest in eighty-five, eighty-seven, eighty-nine and maybe the entire courtyard. our unit picked up speed, realizing that although willie, ski and them wouldn't catch up to us for a little while, we were still trapped between the search and destroy squad from ninety-one and home base. they were closing in quickly and soon would be heard by their side, destroying any chance of a sneak attack.

we were committed, this is what the day had been building to. our commando unit went into action, silently, like a pride of young lions moving in for a strike on some unsuspecting antelope herd, who, although they hadn't spotted the predators, nonetheless could feel the impending danger on the wind.

although justin was the fastest and our hopes held mostly on him, the attack was led by gregory and gary, the twins, who moved in tandem, both confusing and drawing the initial defense of the homebase team. the guards of the homebase, alerted by the growing warning cries of the search and destroy team, went into defensive posture. they were fast, the first wave on the perimeter. the next circle of little brothers who had been put in strategic spots to hold certain positions and to close in if the perimeter was breached, moved in. then there was the inner circle of the slowest who literally formed a chain around the homebase. they had little area to cover and had little to do but guard the prisoners during most of the game. but they knew that when under attack they were the last line of defense.

the attack was a work of art. gregory and gary had drawn a hole in the perimeter and then withdrew, baiting and taking a number of the perimeter guards with them. so busy watching the twins, few had seen russell, douglass and k pot sneak down the avenue and weren't ready for the lightning attack from directly across the street. the three jumped the fence at about the same time and were quickly within only a few feet of homebase before they were discovered.

panic broke out from among the inner circle as they converged on themselves in an attempt to stop this puncture in their defense which was in shambles.

this confusion signaled justin, kevin and dean's final assault. they each ran toward homebase from three different directions. it was with one of the three of them that the captured pinned their hope.

all eyes focused on the three sleek runners, a thing of beauty, watching the three of them swerve, dodge, stop, start and step aside, eluding virtually the entire defense running over itself in bedlam. their carefully planned defense in a state of confusion.

after the three had penetrated the perimeter, the hundred eyes focused. everything stopped and a kind of slow motion dance played itself out. this was the entire game. they each smelled exhilaration in their perspiration. this was what it had all been for and this was all anyone would talk about or remember about the game in the time to come. there was an ever increasing silence as there were fewer and fewer boys left between the three boys and the barrels. the moment of truth had arrived. the few remaining defensive players moved to their final defensive stances.

-ring-o-levio one-two-three

rang out as the decoys were caught, but still the three fastest held their feet. the people on homebase took a collective inhalation, waiting for the touch and the words

-free base, free base

signaling their release from this imposed spell of stillness they had been relegated to since capture earlier.

-ring-o-levio one-two-three

kevin was caught.

-ring-o-levio one-two-three

they converged on dean.

just three defenders stood between justin and the team clutching the homebase barrels. justin suddenly stops, moves to the side, eluding the first, spins a three hundred and sixty going the same way before dancing past the second. just as the last defender commits himself, justin stops, seems almost to give up as if waiting for the inevitable tag. it seems an eternity but just at the moment when it seems there is no way for him not to be tagged he hits the ground, turns and slides into homebase, feet first, yelling

-free base! free base!

the second

-free base!

could hardly be heard amongst the pandemonium that breaks loose. the squeals of freedom signal the wave of running boys as everyone captured escapes. in the near darkness it is almost impossible to recapture anyone.

ninety-one is demoralized. it is nearly sundown and the team of eighty-five, eighty-seven and eighty-nine wins.

thunderclouds open up amidst howls of victory.

fifty/fifty
for me me and lenny

two boys, friends, as only two boys can be, sitting, playing marbles on the second floor landing of the two building brownstone apartment house. they had known each other only this summer, yet they were the closest of friends. instantly. close as only friends at the age of nine can be. friends that only that particular age can bring together. they had become fast friends, easily, overnight. dean's aunt was the super and davinci lived across the hallway or he had since the beginning of summer. dean spent every chance he could over at his aunt's. she had no children, only a grown son somewhere. he and she had had a special relationship since as long as he could remember.

there were only two apartments on a floor. the hallway was lit by a simple single hallway fixture. the two bodies seemed transfixed. still as they were, they merged with the shadows, their heads within inches of one another.

as dean lined up his shot davinci spoke, just above a whisper.

-i'll see you again.

-i know.

-soon.

-i know.

-i, i will.

-i know,

replied dean, not taking his eye off the golden swirled marble at the center of the landing. he aimed his favorite black at the golden swirl. not wanting to talk about it, he didn't want to linger on the topic of davinci's leaving tomorrow.

-i'll see you again.

-i know.

-even if i die.

he shot and missed. the marble rolled listlessly to one side.

-what?

-i know it.

-how?

-somehow.

this was the first time that dean had heard davinci talk about dying. in fact this was the first time he had ever thought about death at all, much less contemplating the death of someone he knew. death was for old, old people or people you didn't know. of course they had discussed the hole in davinci's heart. the concept was still baffling to dean. he could never really fathom it or the correlation between the tiny hole and the sluggishness and slightly bloated look davinci had begun to have. he noticed that davinci breathed heavily these days and lately he had begun to sweat a lot. but then it was august in new york city. what it was that he didn't understand was if the hole had been in his heart all this time, why did they have to operate now? dean's aunt had warned him not to rip and run because davinci had this hole in his heart.

-if i tell you a secret, will you promise not to tell any one?

-cross my heart...

and hope to die just came into dean's mind. it somehow made him feel a little guilty and sad.

-i might die.

his whisper cut across the silence between the two boys.

-doctor told me himself,
i'm not supposed to tell my mother.
she didn't want him to tell me,

but he wanted me to know what was going on.
so i would understand everything and not be afraid.
fifty/fifty.

-what?

-that's what the doctor said, fifty/fifty.

-fifty/fifty? what does that mean?

-means they are gonna try and fix it,
but they don't know if i'm gonna make it.

-how do you know?

-doctor sat me down and explained everything.
that there is a small hole in my heart.
that i was born with it.
it didn't heal like it was supposed to
when i was inside my mother.
that i would continue to get sicker and sicker
unless they opened me up here.

he was pointing to his chest.

-they're gonna open up your chest?

dean was horrified.

-and sew it up.

-won't that hurt?

-i'm gonna be asleep. he told me i won't feel a thing.

-are you scared?

-yeah. sometimes i wake up
in the middle of the night and it's dark.
i can't feel my body and i wonder if i'm dead.
i try to imagine what it would feel like.
i can't.
i close my eyes and lie there and try to feel
what it must be like to feel nothing.
to be nothing.

they're not going to operate for a few days.

-then why you got to go tomorrow?

-so they can get me ready.
i don't know what they're gonna do.
said they gonna watch me for a while,
then they're gonna put me to sleep
and everything will be alright when i wake up.

-yeah?

-if i wake up. if i don't, i guess i'll be dead.

-i didn't know that's where your heart is,

murmured dean, looking at his own chest, not knowing what else to say.

-i thought it was on this side.
but anyway, what does fifty/fifty mean?

-it means fifty/fifty. fifty chances i'll wake up,
and fifty chances i won't.

there was a silence before davinci spoke again.

-it didn't look as if the operation was gonna get done.
we didn't have the money. but the hospital found it.
they said they would take me as soon as a bed opened up.
they called last night.

-i'm gonna miss you.

-me too.

-you're my best friend.

the two boys looked into each other's eyes. they felt the strength of their bond and the purity of their love.

the door to davinci's apartment opened and it was apparent to dean that davinci's mother had been crying.

-it's time for davinci to come in.
he has to rest before...tomorrow.

say goodnight to dean.

-bye davinci, see you soon.

-see you later, okay? remember, no matter what.

the door was just about to close when suddenly davinci came back out into the hallway again. he handed dean the bag full of golden swirled marbles.

-hold on to this for me, for the next time.
i feel better knowing that you have them, just in case.

it was the last image dean would have, standing there alone in the hallway, holding the golden swirled marbles. he would always remember the look on davinci's face, as the door slowly closed.

----

it wasn't until the next week when dean returned to his aunt's that he found out. no one talked about it. the bag full of golden swirled marbles lay upon the kitchen window sill, just as he had left them. finally he grabbed the bag and walked across the hall. he knocked on davinci's door. he waited. there was no answer.

it was then he knew it would never be the same again. davinci was gone. at nine. death had come amongst them as quietly as an early morning snow, had descended like an early sunset in winter, an early frost, leaving him cold, alone and somehow shut out from everybody and everything else he had ever known. he could trust life no more. he had no way to resolve this loss of innocence.

death had come and he had hardly noticed it. everything was changed, forever and yet he seemed almost the same. but something was different. it was his first taste of the sadness of life, an end to childhood. there was an emptiness, a void which could not be filled, a loneliness which would never be answered, a sadness which would never go away.

he felt a stranger. shut out. totally alone. there were no tears. death meant no one on the other side of the door. no davinci. a best friend gone forever. he tried to imagine just where he had gone, where he was now. he had nothing. he walked slowly back to his aunt's, barely aware of anyone or anything around him, numbed by the enormity of infinity and the eternity of forever. left empty with a bag full of golden swirled marbles.

----

it would be twenty-nine years later before the words davinci had spoken would reappear in his mind. standing on a subway platform at two on a summer morning, he remembered...

-even if i die

resurfaced as memories sometimes do, unsolicited, silently, without warning. dean looked at the stranger's face and saw davinci's eyes. before they had even met he knew they would be friends, forever.

★ ★ ★

coming upon malcolm
for the man who created knuckles

icy cold, red hook february afternoon. the boy could take the cold no longer. toes and fingers frozen stiff finally overcame the eleven-year old need to play and run, not wanting to waste the sunshine and the freedom of a sunday afternoon.

as he opened the door of the third floor apartment he could feel the heavy prolonged silence. making the obligatory turn into the kitchen, he found his father at the table, sitting shoulders slumped, head in hand.

the small black and white television which sat on the counter played. his mother stood, arms folded, looking intently into the screen as some newscaster recanted details.

the boy quietly walked further into the kitchen. it was then that he noticed the small involuntary jerks of his father's back. he moved closer before he realized his father was crying.

the world had changed. his father was crying. it was a concept he had never conceived. it was something he would see only once again, within the year, at the funeral of the one woman his father called ma.

the boy looked to his mother. she didn't turn. she said softly, simply

      -they killed malcolm x. the bastards.

          ★ ★ ★

city line

sister/sister
for tini

the sisters came through the door like a wind gaining speed.
each surveyed the smaller rooms and each drew her own
conclusion.   each sister went in a different direction,
thoroughly taking in each and every detail for future
retelling.   each talking, nonstop.   in this never-ending
chorale, they each spoke and listened all at once.   one communal voice, demanding, searching, berating and healing at
the same time, leaving no possibility of silence.

> –sister, sister, no food in the ice box, the dishes
> ain't been washed.

> –sister, sister, the beds ain't been made, this place is a mess.

> –sister, sister, at least the children are clean,
> but lord these heads ain't been combed in days.

> –sister, sister, you should see what's in the bathroom.

upon assuring their collective self that he was not on the
premises, they turned as one on quiet sister who had sat at
the table and silently watched this unusual commando assault

team. led by big sister, tall, red bone and crowned with stunning premature silver hair which emphasized her birthright as the eldest, she was followed closely by fighting sister who commanded respect. everyone knew of her temper. her eyes stretched wide and she seemed to grow blacker as she grew angrier. the revealment of the whites usually meant yours was next in a long line of asses she had had to kick in her life. she was followed by talking sister whose weapon was her tongue. she could talk you to death and back. she could talk until you prayed for the release of your everlasting soul with the fervent promise to never do again whatever it was you had done, if she would only stop talking. the rear was brought up by baby sister who was tough. she just didn't care. she would say whatever was on her mind to anyone and she could beat everyone except fighting sister.

> -sister, sister, what must we do?
> we can't leave her here.

> -the black bastard!

> -i'll get the children. come on here.
> one of you find me a comb and brush.

> -lord, have mercy.

> -sister, sister, you've got to see the bathroom.

they all stood still, silent, legs akimbo, hands on hips, mouths open, aghast, as they surveyed the damage in the tub. it was the first silence since they had entered the small apartment. in fact it was the first time in years the sisters were speechless.

-sister, sister, uhm, uhm, uhm!

-lord have mercy.

-sister, sister, have you ever seen such a mess in your life?

-the black bastard!

what seemed to be every piece of clothing in the house, except what was on the backs of the children and quiet sister, was floating in a tub full of water.

-i told him i was going to leave.
he said not if i didn't have anything to wear.

spoke quiet sister for the first time since they had arrived, pulling her blue bathrobe tight around her neck.

-don't you worry about anything, sister's here now.

-the black bastard! i'd like to get my hands
around his throat!

the sisters went into action. heads were combed, clothes dried, bags packed, children dressed and fed. the sisters pieced together something for quiet sister to wear. it was as she changed that fighting sister saw the marks on quiet sister's body. big sister gave her a blouse, talking sister gave her the blue and white suit she had packed for church sunday, fighting sister gave her shoes, as she was the only one with feet large enough and baby sister gave her stockings as she was the right color. by early evening the car was packed and everything was in order for a quick getaway.

fighting sister sat down.

-sister, sister, don't you think it's time we got on the road?
we got a long drive ahead of us.

-i ain't setting foot outside this house.
i'm gonna wait for this fool.
i ain't leaving until i try my damndest to send the bastard back to hell.
he want to hit somebody?
i got something for his ass!

there was a little grumbling, but fighting sister had made up her mind and as she was driving there really was very little else to do. one by one the sisters sat down and waited.

they sat in silence but a brief time before talking sister took up the thread and in a short while had woven the fabric of the conversation so that everyone soon joined in. everyone but quiet sister who sat secure in her family as the cacophony picked up speed.

the children were asleep and big sister had just begun to doze when they heard him trying to put his key in the door. fighting sister had put the chain on and in his stupor he couldn't quite figure out what was wrong.

-sister, sister, take the children into the bedroom and
close the door. don't wake them up.

-no, sister, sister, take them out the back door
and put them in the car.
they shouldn't see any of this.

-who put the goddamn latch on?

-i did, you black bastard!

-what you all doing setting up in my house for?

-waiting for your sorry black ass to come home!

he kicked the door, ripping the latch from the frame and strode into the house.

-nobody keeps me out of my house!
what you waiting on me for, anyway?

-'cause i'm fixing to send your sorry black ass
back to hell!

and with that fighting sister jumped across the coffee table, and punched him dead in his eye. she popped a right jab into his upper lip and a left cross to his jaw. baby sister came in from the side and kneed him in the stomach. big sister supervised as talking sister started right on in slashing him with razor like comments, drawing blood.

the attack was sudden and carried out with the precision of a tactical detail. it didn't take much time, he was already drunk.

after he fell she wrapped her hands around his neck and tried to squeeze the living daylights out of him.

fighting sister had to be pulled off.

-you black bastard!
if you ever come within sight of my sister
or if i ever lay eyes on your sorry black ass again,
i swear to god, i'll put you in the ground!

not in the eight days it took him to recover, nor anytime after he left the hospital or through the many years when connection between father and children was tenuously restored, not until his body was laid in its grave did he ever attempt to contact, talk to or lay eyes upon quiet sister again.

★ ★ ★

done
for charlene

it was finished.

the calls had been made, returned and accepted. the food
had been shopped for, brought, cleaned and prepared. as she
stood staring out of the window her husband and son ritu-
alistically built the fire on the grill. she silently went over the
menu again, checking for even the slightest detail that might
have been overlooked.

the chicken was fried, the potato salad made, collard greens
done, candied sweet potatoes ready to go into the oven, just
to brown the marshmallow topping, as were the rolls. the
hamburgers and hot-dogs sat on the table awaiting the
lighting of the grill and the arrival of the children. the ribs
were seasoned. of course the corn pudding was sitting,
cooling on the stove, it was her specialty. the string beans
were cooked with smoked turkey for her non-pork-eating
daughter. the macaroni and cheese had just been taken out
so she could pop it in to brown five minutes before they sat
down to eat. the corn, okra and tomato sat covered on the
counter, alongside a small pot of turnips. in the refrigerator,
the green salad sat next to the tomato, onion and cucumber,

coleslaw and pickled beets. on the shelf below sat the shrimp salad. below that were desserts, her blueberry and cherry cobblers and three of her homemade pound cakes on the counter. in the freezer, strawberry, vanilla and her favorite, black walnut ice cream. the bottom of the refrigerator was filled with beer. the bar was stocked with every kind of liquor as well as a new green plastic outdoor garbage can filled with ice, soda and beer. the pina coladas and the whiskey sours were ready to be made, the ingredients and blender were on the little table outside the window. plastic knives, forks, spoons and bags, paper plates, cups, napkins were all mentally checked off.

she surveyed the yard. it had been fastidiously prepared. the lawn manicured so even a barber would approve. the outdoor lawn furniture was new. the two card tables set up, four new decks of pinochle cards, one blue and one red on each of the tables, pads and pens ready. the lawn sparkled in the sun of the spring afternoon. she looked at the cloudless blue sky and knew that god had answered her prayer. it was a perfect day.

as she crossed from the kitchen toward the stairs she surveyed her house. every room was finally as she wanted it. all new furniture, bought within the last six months. the bay windows in the living room were finally in. the new carpet had been laid only two weeks before. every surface gleamed. the nook in every cranny was filled.

she stood and admired her handicraft. she was complete. she

smiled and that smile carried her up the stairs to the master bedroom at the end of the hall. the entire house was immaculate. she had earned that smile. she had worked hard to get it to this point. she felt pride and joy. she alone knew the struggle to get here. she had time to leisurely draw a bath, soak and do the nails on her hands and feet. she then did her face, hair and dressed. she slowly slipped on her sandals as she heard the first car pull up. she recognized the voices of her sister and family before she heard the doorbell.

----

she surveyed the table at dinner. everyone had arrived, three sisters, two brothers, two brother-in-laws, two sister-in-laws, three of her four children as her oldest hadn't gotten home from school, her one grandchild, seven nieces, nine nephews, two great nieces, one great nephew, two cousins, her two closest friends and their children. her husband was engaged in conversation with her youngest sister's husband and her youngest brother. her husband had never looked happier.

everyone was laughing, eating, enjoying themselves. it was the culmination of a perfect meal. a great time had by all. after the perfect meal she washed the dishes and served dessert. everyone settled down to cobbler, cake and ice cream. so much of a good time was being had that no one noticed when she quietly slipped off upstairs.

they had almost missed her when she appeared dressed impeccably in a blue traveling suit, bag and shoes, complete

with matching luggage. she waited atop the stairs. her eldest
daughter's eyes were the first to meet hers. she recognized
the women in the eyes of this her womanchild who had
months before given her her first grandchild. she had crossed
the bridge in giving birth and they had come to understand
one another. next were the eyes of her sister closest in age
to her, her face forming a silent question. no one else
noticed until talking sister finally looked up and asked,

-when did you get that? i like it.
the color looks good on you.

in a very loud voice. one by one they all turned to see the
stunning figure atop the stairs. she waited. only when everything else in the room had literally come to a halt did he feel
the silence. she waited. he interrupted his attention from the
television and turned his eyes from the play-offs.
she waited. he looked into her eyes and still she waited until
she was sure he knew. it was only then, when she had seen
the look in his eyes, it was at that moment she descended the
newly carpeted stairs of her immaculate and perfect house
for the last time.

she kept her gaze trained on him through all the confusion,
as the family gathered around for what most of them thought
was just an impromptu fashion show. he knew. amidst the
applause and questioning glances, he knew. he knew it was
for all those times, when she had been pregnant, when she
had been mothering. he knew it was for all the other
women, over all the years. she had said nothing and he knew
that now it was too late.

he had settled down over the last seven years. they were finally financially stable. she had everything she had ever wanted, but he knew she had not forgotten or forgiven.

there was surprise when the taxi-cab drove up and honked. there was little time for most to comprehend. she had kissed all those she would by the time the matching set of luggage had been placed in the trunk of the waiting taxi-cab.

she didn't even look at him as she walked through the door. she was gone. without looking back she threw up a hand. she had not said a word for there was no need to say goodbye.

★ ★ ★

bubblegum
for zechariah, jeremiah and nehemiah
the three prophets

the adults were so busy talking that no one noticed the
little boy set out from the unfamiliar steps of his aunt's row
house in west philadelphia. clutching four pennies in his
hand, he walked unhesitantly down to the corner. after
carefully looking in both directions, he crossed the street
into the gas station on the triangular block. there in front
of him was the object of his trek, the round domed
bubblegum machine.

he reached up and carefully inserted one of the pennies into
the little metal slot. it held the penny up in place. he then
reached for the little silver handle and twisted it one whole
turn to the right. the entire mass of bubblegum shifted,
slightly and he could hear one piece of bubblegum fall. he
pushed open the little swinging door on the hinge and
retrieved a piece of blue bubblegum. he was pleased, it was
his favorite.

he was as intrigued with the workings of the bubblegum
machine as he was with the bubblegum itself and
whenever he had any pennies on him, he would get an

older cousin or an adult to take him to get bubblegum. it was because he had done this so often that he was sure he could do it on his own. today's solo journey was his first.

so pleased that all had gone so well, he crossed the street again. basking in the glow of his oncoming maturity this venture would demonstrate to his family, he started down the side of the triangular block. engrossed as he was in his own thoughts, it was only when white people began to pass him that he realized that suddenly the sunny day had darkened under the shade of hugh trees overhead. it was then that he noticed that the street had widened and that traffic had picked up considerably. he looked around him and the street did not look familiar at all.

at that moment he realized that he was totally lost. it never occurred to him to simply turn around and retrace his steps. by the time he did look around, where he had come from looked no more familiar than where he was going.

the little boy did not panic, but he was scared. he was lost. this was the one thing you tried very hard not to do and here he was, stupid enough to have gotten himself lost. he began to perspire just enough to begin to melt the blue off of the four pieces of bubblegum he held in his left hand.

he had just come to the conclusion that he was going to have to ask someone for help. he was trying to rectify his mother's most important edict to never talk to strangers when he saw the policeman.

without a doubt he was the biggest white man he had ever seen. the policeman noticed the tears beginning to roll down his face and asked him if he was lost. he remembered his mother's admonition that if he was ever lost go up to the nearest policeman and tell him so. after a moment's hesitation he made a decision and for the first time in his life the little black boy spoke to somebody white.

he told the policeman his name, that he lived at 85 lorraine street, apt 6b in brooklyn, new york. that he was here, in philadephia with his mother visiting with her sister. her name was aunt mable. she lived just a block from where he had walked to get the bubblegum, which he then showed the policeman. he did not know her address or the name of the street. he did know his telephone number at home in new york and he was lost.

after pondering the situation for a minute, the policeman called into the station house. deciding that the little boy should be brought in, the policeman took the boy on his first ride in a police car. he would only ever experience two in his life, both today.

once in the station they took him into a curiously empty room with two desks and a phone and called his father, in new york. his father, who worked the third shift at the post office, was asleep and understandably upset upon learning that the police had his only son in custody. he was frustrated at the realization that he didn't know his sister in law's telephone number or address, as his wife had taken the address book with her to philadelphia and mad with himself that he couldn't remember his sister-in-law's last name. anyone he could think of to call for the number was already in philadelphia at his wife's family reunion and he was infuriated that somehow his wife, running her damn mouth, he surmised, had managed to lose their four-year old son.

the police then decided to ride the little boy around the neighborhood where they picked him up. the little boy sat in the back, his little head just barely visible.

it was one of his aunt's neighbors who recognized the little head in the police car's backseat window. she flagged down the police car, screaming the entire time for his aunt. his mother, who by this time was convinced that she had lost her only child and would never see her baby again, had all but collapsed.

returning from the near dead, his mother ran out to meet him and gathered him into her arms where she swore he would never get a chance to get away again. in response to her continuous questioning, the little boy began to tell his mother of his misfortunes. showing her the melted candy in his blue hand, he explained getting lost, talking to the white policeman, his two rides in the police car and the call home to his father.

she was so grateful at having him again in her arms that she forgot to be angry. as happy as she was at seeing him, she dreaded the next conversation with his father. she could

face that now because her child was back in her embrace.
it was his aunt nina that suggested the dog harness. as his
cousins sat around laughing at him tied to the livingroom
steps for the next hour, he ate all four pieces of blue
bubblegum and refused to speak or to share his well-earned
treasure with any of them.

★ ★ ★

proposal
for zakiyyah

the sisters stood together, blossoms clustered across the open field. the beauty of the women, collectively, stood out. the blessings of *ramadan* had been received, as the month of fasting ended. the feasting which accompanied the *eid* celebration had just begun. the finery of the community was in full bloom as the sisters stood in clusters, talking, a year of living to catch up on.

the brothers strode from one group of brothers to another. they began to gather at the front of the field, carrying instruments. their intention of giving praise evident.

the children ran, enjoying themselves, immersed in play. this was a great day; food and friends. they too felt the blessings shared, as the restraints of the past month were released. they could look around and see the community revel in its power.

completion of the fast indeed brought its rewards, in ways immediately felt. there was a sense of victory, of having completed the mission, a sense of strength felt individually as well as collectively. the feast was well deserved.

fathers strode across the open field proudly carrying sons too young to walk on their backs and shoulders, holding the hands of sons too young to run.

mothers watched daughters play, holding babies needing to nurse.

the group of mothers consisted of friends, found through islam, most of whom saw each other only a few times a year. occasionally there would be couplings of best friends.

basima watched the group of girls playing. each of the sisters around her had a daughter within three years of each other. they watched them play, kimars blowing in the wind. there was kubcha, tarika, suhilo, shereka, basia, nzinga, najah, khadijah and zakiyyah. basima watched as the multi-colored kufi on the little golden brother continually circled the gold and blue of her daughter's kimar.

the brothers stood apart. the circle of men grew steadily as more and more brothers drifted toward the clearing under the trees where the prayers had been led. drums and other supporting instruments slowly appeared as they prepared to anoint the breaking of the fast with musical offerings.

-as salaamu alaikum,

rang out time and time again as another would join the growing swarm of brothers.

-wa alaikum as salaam,

returned the chorus of voices, as brothers hugged and spoke on the passage of time since they had last greeted one another. brothers congratulated brothers on births and new marriages. some of the brothers knew each other only from *eid* celebrations. some had traveled from as far away as atlanta to make *eid* in prospect park in brooklyn. the park teamed with the energy of the islamic community as it showcased itself at its finest.

brothers were adorned in kufis of all colors, as were the heads of their sons. the little brothers walked erect, aware of their new clothing, their importance as children in this event and in the community.

saeed watched his eldest son play. his three daughters were with their mother where he had just returned their infant son to feed. he watched the multi-colored kufi of his son as he ran, in what seemed never ending circles, at the far end of the field. he took no notice until his wife commented on the little girl in the gold and blue kimar in the middle of the circle.

the little brown skinned sister seemed to pay the little golden boy no mind. he jumped, he climbed trees, swung from limbs, performed cartwheels, walked on his hands and ran races in his attempt to attract her attention. it was his conversation that finally grabbed her interest. engrossed in conversation, they were suddenly oblivious to the roving bands of kufis and the little brothers underneath them.

it was later that afternoon that the little brother approached his father with his request. he was quite serious, as seven sometimes warrants. he asked if his father might speak to hers. he felt that he had found his helpmate, his love. he wanted to offer the little brown skinned sister in the gold and blue kimar a proposal, for the time when they would come of age. he had made his decision. the father looked down into the serious eyes of his seven year old son, as he pointed out the sister in the gold and blue kimar. in this he was adamant.

the father smiled as he approached the brothers.

-as salaamu alaikum

-wa alaikum asalaam

-brother, may i have a word with you?
my son, it seems, has been taken with your daughter.

-my daughter,

laughed the father,

-but she's only six years old.

-my son is seven. he has asked me to ask you to consider him
 as a possible son-in-law when they both come of age.

-it's really not up to me,

smiled the father of the little brown skinned sister, as he looked out in the field near his wife. he located the gold and blue kimar and saw for himself the golden boy in the multi-colored kufi who was balancing a stick in his palm. even from this distance he could see his daughter laughing.

-well, it looks as if they're getting along pretty well.
i expected this one day, but not quite so soon,

laughed the father, as he watched his proposed son-in-law.

-this is her first proposal. we shall see. in sha'llah.

-in sha'llah.

the sisters laughed as they heard of the proposal. careful though not to laugh when the serious young brother came within earshot. they were touched.

-well at least someone is still interested in love.

-if i was seven i'd snatch him up.

-well some mother done raised him well.

-al hum du li lah.

in between their laughter they commended the little brother for his focus, his planning for the future. they warned the mother of the daughter to watch him carefully, that she had better keep an eye. they commended the maturity of the sender of such a proposal through channels and wondered at the potential of such a resourceful and serious young brother, while commenting on how adorable he and his proposal were and how cute. news of the proposal traveled along the laughter all afternoon.

the little brown skinned sister just laughed when she heard of the proposal from her mother later that evening. this was the earliest proposal received by anyone in the six generations since ibo landing.

at six she had no plans for marriage. truthfully the thought had never even crossed her mind. but she would take his offer and give it some careful thought for about fifteen minutes, which was as long as her six-year old spirit could hold anything.

it was only the little golden brother in the multi-colored kufi who knew the true extent and sincerity of his love. he had seen what he needed. he would talk seriously to no other girl. from that day on, he considered himself engaged. he alone knew the commitment of his soul. he alone knew that it would resurface when they would come to the age of marriage.

★ ★ ★

beyond

angels?
for my best friend

the two friends stood alongside the road, their figures stark against the expansive snow clouds which covered the sunlight. staring silently, the soft whiteness which was beginning to envelope them gave everything a certain unreal, dream-like quality. wind blew gusts of snow into their faces. trucks flew along at incredible speeds, sending off sprays of slush, with near lethal intensities. the brutal february sky slowly edged toward the darkness of its colorless sunset.

    -oooohhh budddyyy!!! it's fuckin' cold out here!

guy's teeth were beginning to chatter, as short bursts of breath appeared from behind his rainbow colored scarf, twice wrapped securely, desperately, around his face.

    -well, if the cold don't get us, the klan probably will,

murmured his best friend.

        -always the optimist, eh?

retorted guy.

        -shit, my hands are freezing,

returned his best friend.

his fingers were beginning to crack from holding the cardboard sign, with its magic marker printing.

there had been quite a discussion the night before as the colors were chosen. purple and yellow were finally decided on, partly because they looked good together and as colors they would stand out. the ritual of making a sign the night before had been enacted. both friends knew the value of a good sign. it could mean the difference of hours in your arrival time, to say nothing of the quality of your rides. this sign with its ohio on one side and cleveland on the other had begun to show the fatigue of the journey. the edges had begun to bend and the wind had beat up the cardboard sign that looked ever so small against the darkening sky.

guy could feel the cold, even through his fur-lined gloves.

-and we're only in fuckin' west virginia

lamented his best friend through the ten feet of metallic blue scarf that wrapped itself around his head and upper body, covering most of his army green hawk-fighter and its hood.

-oh, shit,

cried guy, as the wind began to play havoc with the sign,

-be careful this wind don't blow you into one of those trucks. these suckers ain't playing around.

the warning came none too soon, for just then a tractor trailer came barreling along at about sixty-five or seventy miles per hour and nearly pulled both friends into the road after it.

-this ain't no place to catch a ride. this ain't even no fuckin' place to stand,

yelled guy through clinched teeth.

-this is like a truck route or something.

mumbled his best friend, whose teeth were seriously beginning to chatter.

-shit!

guy took the sign and stuck it under his arm and began to walk along the shoulder as far away from the edge of the road as he could. silently his best friend turned and followed directly behind him, keeping an ever-present eye out behind them as they walked. the wind blew. neither could remember the last time they had seen a car or a possible ride. only trucks, followed by tractor trailers, followed by double-decker buses or the occasional trailer cradling new car models to the city. not that one couldn't get a ride with the occasional trucker, each flying down the road faster than the other, but here there was no place for anyone to stop, especially in this snow and ice.

-this is incredible, i've never seen anything like this.
-these fools ain't playin', not one bit! they're moving!!!

-that motherfucker knew exactly what he was doing,
leaving us on this road.

guy was referring to the previous hitch who had left them in
a place impossible to catch another ride.

-motherfucker. look at us fools, we could get killed out here.

-i know one thing, this particular fool is colddd!!

-we better find a ride soon.

-yeah right, from where?

-well, i tell you buddy, we better find somewhere to get
warm soon or we're going to freeze our fuckin' black asses off
out here!

it was true, they hadn't seen anywhere that even remotely
looked like a good place to catch a ride in miles. no rest areas,
scenic picnic overviews or even enough shoulder to stand on,
much less somewhere a truck or even a car could slow down,
stop and safely pick up two, at best, questionabe looking
characters. at this rate they would be walking to ohio.

then again, if anyone looked at them good, they would find
these two hard to resist. they had too much magic about them.

they looked comical, somehow safe. anyone who stopped for them usually felt better, for having spent time in their company when they dropped them off, because usually they had had such a good time laughing.

these two were old friends, who loved life, loved living life and loved living life in each other's company as often as life allowed. they always had a good time together. anyone caught in the web of their laughter found it infectious.

truthfully, in the past, they had had unprecedented hitching karma. each of them had good hitching karma alone but together they were insurmountable. they beat train and bus schedules. they were known for stepping out of guy's best friend's house in jamaica, queens to go to the store for eggs and ending up eating a late brunch in guy's house in new haven, connecticut. their fastest time was somewhere well under two hours, door to door, on a weekday morning. indeed it was because of this hitching karma in the past that they found themselves on the road to cleveland this time.

-we should never have hitched from philadelphia.

-yeah right! you can say that again! who hitches from one no place to another,

laughed guy.

-we should have gone back to new york and left from there, we would be there by now.

-yeah, buddy, but that shit ain't goin' to do us
a bit of good out here, on this highway,
in this cold, at this time!
in fact, we ain't even goin' to get there today,
so we better think about where the fuck
we are goin' to spend the night.

it had begun to snow in earnest. so lost in their own mis-
ery were the two friends that they hadn't noticed the red
van go by and stop about a hundred yards or so up ahead,
where it had managed to find a little turnoff. the van
turned and that was when the friends noticed the two head-
lights riding up slowly in the distance. they immediately
became suspicious.

-this could be it,

whispered his best friend, as he began to look for some trees.

-anything strange jump off and i'm headed straight for that,

said guy, as he pointed to a large clearing in a nearby patch of woods,
but then they both knew in this new snow they would be ripe tar-
gets for anyone. they both knew that if they had to make a run for
it in west virginia, they were in trouble. they both knew that if anyone went after them in this weather, it was for keeps. they both
knew...

the new snow had begun to stick. the carlights slowed.

-we're fucked now!

the shape of this old van slowly became visible in the falling snow. ever so slowly a window rolled down and both friends felt the hair on the back of their necks stand on edge.

this could be it, the moment that all afrikan american males face at some time in their young adult lives. the moment when you feel the heat and heart of the ancestors' breath upon your face and beating within your chest. the sound of escaped slavery floods into the memory of your inner ear, your breathing becomes short and ragged, your palms begin to sweat, your stomach sinks and you feel your knees begin to buckle just a little. your eyes strain, your fists clinch, you come up onto the balls of your feet and you are prepared to run, fight or drop to the ground.

a silent prayer volunteers itself up and you are ready to take that stand for your life.

in many ways this is what your life has been spent preparing for, the hours of playing war, the massive ring-o-levio games. for this one great battle, the one you constantly prepare for in the hope you never have to wage. and you think,

-what a stupid place to die.

-they'll never even find my body until the spring.
.
-what the hell are we doing out here anyway?

that's what you say and you know that's what they'll ask.
a west virginian twang rang out,

> -hey, y'all need a ride? this is a helluva place
> to try to catch a ride.

the two friends climbed into the back. silently watching
each other as they answered questions. the van was occu-
pied by about six or seven long-haired people and the
unmistakable smell of herb.

a sense of relief spread over the two friends as they moved
into that familiar space. it was the early seventies, the war in
vietnam still polarized the country. it was a time when
crewcuts meant redneck and long hair meanst hippy. the
two friends happily recognized their hippy brethren. they
were among fellow heads and were being given free passage.
they gratefully shared some of their stash with the six or
seven long-haired west virginian hippies.

> -this is not a good place to be tryin' to catch a ride.
> where y'all tryin' to get to?

asked the driver. he looked nordic, with golden, shoulder-
length hair and a comforting smile.

> -cleveland.

said guy, with just a trace of malice in his voice.
> -you're a fuckin' long way from cleveland.

laughed another voice from the back of the van.

-and don't think we don't know that,

added guy, with a look that got him a long laugh all around.

-where y'all coming from,

asked one of the two females, the one with the long golden hair in the front seat of the van.

-phillie, since eight this morning,

moaned his best friend, still trying to warm his hands.

-you're lucky it was us come along
and not some of the hollitt boys!

-and don't think we don't know that, too!

repeated guy to another round of laughter.

-y'all live in phillie?-

queries the blond female, from the back of the van.
-new york,

both friends said, simultaneously.

-what's it like to live there?

asked the girl up front.

> -like any place else, with folks that are good
> and folks that are fucked-up,

laughed guy.

> -you play?

asked the tall quiet bearded brown-haired mountain man from the back. he refered to guy's flute case, which was tied round his shoulder with a bright purple sash. the mountain man was holding a twelve-string acoustic guitar.

> -yeah, i play,

answered guy, graciously.

> -what kind of music?

> -my own and lots of different music.

> -jazz?

> -some.

> -i love jazz!

> -oh yeah?

asked guy, as he shot his best friend a look.

> -who do you like?

-well, coryell and mcglaughlin, santana and of course jimi.

his best friend knew that they had him, now. someone had mentioned hendrix and that was the magic password for guy.

-wanna play something?

asked the guitarist, as he softly hit the first chords to *castles made of sand.*

-i would but my fingers are still frozen.
is there any place around here where we could crash for the
night? a motel? a holiday inn?
shit, i'm tired and we sure ain't gonna make cleveland tonight.

-there's the one over on route 36
and it'll be easy to get a ride in the morning.

-thanks a lot.

-we'll drop you over there.

-we appreciate it.

-no problem, just light up another one of those
new york city joints, will you?

-gratefully, no problem.

and guy proceeded to roll.

-hey,

as the guitarist strummed a few chords,

-that's *castles made of sand*, ain't it?

and guy took out his flute and played.

it was almost midnight before they were dropped off. it wasn't until they were laying in bed that night at the holiday inn, that his best friend asked him,

-yo guy, if they hadn't come along,
do you think we would have died?

he grunted some non-committal sound as he drifted off towards sleep.

-yo guy, think they were angels?

what he could not know was angels were descending, over the entire lewis family, in preparation. his grandmother, big mama, was failing. she would pass in two days. angels were descending, drawing near.

★ ★ ★

going home
for big mama

she lifted gently, easily, separating from the coil. hers was a life over, completed and well done.

------

big mama passed in philadelphia, that winter.

the news reverberating across phone lines, criss-crossing the northeastern seaboard and spreading outward in an ever-widening circle, centered from staunton, a little shenandoah valley town in the blue ridge mountains of virginia.

mable grey lee bertha fannie anne lou ella may franklin lewis was dead.

----

her new astral body took some time to get used to; the weightless-ness, the freedom, the enlarged perception, the ability to be in more than one place at the same time.

----

we, the people of the blue ridge mountains, bury our people in a way passed on through generations.

her body would be taken back home by train, for there was no question that she would be buried in the red clay cemetery across from the old methodist church in cedar green, next to popa.

her children decided that they would accompany the body home on the same train. arranging the time, two daughters and a son boarded in new york city. they were met, in philadelphia, by two more daughters and in washington dc by yet another daughter. an entourage of grandchildren also accompanied the body.

the train arrived in the valley at three thirty that morning. the body was met by the rest of the family and kenneth vaughn who had prepared every lewis body for burial that any one could remember.

after the family had reviewed kenneth vaughn's preparations and had had time alone with her themselves, mable grey lee bertha fannie anne lou ella may franklin lewis was laid in state and the people of staunton came to pay their respects.

the wake served as a prelude, a dress rehearsal for the main ceremony which would take place the next day.

the food had begun to arrive soon after the news of her death had reached the valley. each neighbor donated their best dish for all the people who would come to the house to offer condolences during these three days and for the reception that would follow the funeral and the burial.

on that cold friday morning, the sun shone brightly. by nine o'clock most of the family had arrived to the largest compound, uncle earl's, the house on bagby street. by the time the minister arrived at nine thirty to deliver the prayer, kenneth vaughn and his deputies were already lining up the cars, arranging, constantly checking and rechecking the list of names, the number of cars needed and the order in which the family would ride to the funeral.

after the prayer circle, kenneth vaughn begins the load in from his list: the eldest son and his wife, the oldest daughter and her husband, the second daughter and the second son, as both were without spouses, first car; third daughter and her husband, fourth daughter and her husband, third son and his wife, second car; fifth daughter and her husband and on and on until all seven daughters and four sons, the remaining eleven who had survived of the thirteen children birthed by mable grey lee bertha fannie anne lou ella may franklin lewis and their spouses were seated in the order of their birth.

next her grandchildren and their mates were loaded, grouped by age. the first six of the forty-one grandchildren filled the seventeenth car, and the great great grandchildren continued at car twenty-three. then began the cars holding her first cousins and so on. there was no accurate count on the number of cars leaving the compound, as everyone lost count after about twenty-six.

the family traveled slowly to the church in cedar green. cars traveling in both directions stop for funerals in staunton. even the white people came out of their places of business and stood in reverence as the motorcade passed by. they had heard that miss mable, matriarch to the lewis clan, was being buried today.

the funeral entourage snaked along majestically, eventually winding its way slowly to the church door, where it waited silently until every car had arrived, before each family member deliberately took their place in line, women on the right. the family and kenneth vaughn made a final check, before beginning the processional.

the lewis family looked around and took stock of itself. the family looked good. the offspring of mable grey lee bertha fannie anne lou ella may franklin lewis looked good. this was her finest moment and there was no doubt in the hearts of the family that she was looking down smiling, well pleased.

----

and she was. well pleased. the intensity of the mourning anchored her here. the law of attraction would not have allowed her to leave, even if she had wanted to.

----

the organ music's first strains peeled as the doors were opened and the waiting congregation stood as one. the

homegoing ceremony had begun. the first woman's wail
released as soon as the family hit the door. down the aisle,
heads bowed, slowly walked the entire lewis clan. the enormous family filed in, filling, pew by pew, both sides of the
inner sanctuary. by the time they were all seated, mourning
raged full force.

the entire community had turned out. the little wooden
church was packed to brimming. there was something very
tribal, very old, ancient, about the proceedings. this respect
and reverence shown toward miss lewis was testament of
their approval for the life she had lived. they were there to
recognize the life of one of its most senior and respected
members. there was a sense of celebration at and for the
completion of that life well done. the appreciation of a mission completed, a river crossed over. they each prayed for
as fine a leaving for themselves.

she had not believed in missing church. she had sat in the
front pew every sunday morning her later life just as she had
when she had been raising her family. she had only started
to miss here in the last few years, when her health had
begun failing. even when she had moved in with her children on her farewell family tour she had never forgotten the
church, nor they she.

her family was testament of a mantle that had not been laid
down but had been carried to journey's end and passed on.
there was no doubt that every child, grandchild or great
grandchild raised lewis knew that they had come from some
place and had still somewhere to go.

after the invocation, the ancient choir *sang sweet hour of prayer*, the hymn of faith. it was one of her favorites. there was the reading of the scriptures, old and new testaments, the prayer of comfort and the hymn of consolation, followed by the acknowledgments, resolutions and the reading of the obituary.

----

listening to the obituary being read, she was amazed at her ability to remember everything in her life and she had lived a life.

she had loved a man, walter lewis, had borne him thirteen children, had buried two of them: leroy, her heart, her first born, whom she had until he was nineteen. she could see all his life, his birth, his first suckling in her arms and how he had lain in the snow his last night, hit over the head by assailants, white and unknown. she never got over that night, or her little baby lucy who had got the fever and was gone too soon.

she had almost left them that time, in search of her baby gone. she followed the smell of baby blankets, until she found the white blanket trimmed in green which held her scent. she would not let it go. she carried it as she listened for gurglings in the night. she could not sleep, whenever she heard crying, milk would leak from breasts hard and sore.

at night she would walk around in the dark, finding comfort only from the great tree in the front yard at the top of the hill. it was her oldest friend. she would throw herself at the base of the tree, as she had as a child and there she would rock and rock the empty blanket to sleep.

she left. might never have come back, but the lord allowed her to feel life again, kicking within.

she looked down upon them all, she could only count blessings.

----

as the family sat there, each and every one of them had a different memory of big mama. one grandson remembered her magnificent breakfasts. another grandson remembered her half moon apple pies which she cooked every year before the fair at montgomery park; another grandson recalled the time she had asked him to pick out which chickens would be sunday dinner and had him watch as she wrung their necks and cut off their heads. he remembered always the chickens' death dance, watching their life's blood cascading out. he would never view another sunday dinner the same. a granddaughter remembered getting her hair braided, big mama had no time for the tender-headed; another granddaughter recalled her warm, musky smell and still another scratching her back, which big mama truly loved; a daughter thought of big mama and she eating chitterlings refried in egg; another sitting watching the stories with mama in the afternoon, eating salted tomatoes; a son, the conversations on the porch with mama and her father, daddy franklin, swatting flies in the afternoon; another son watching fireflies at night, with the children running around in the yard trying to catch them; one daughter her smile, still another her laugh and each remembered her arms, for it was within her hugs that she dispensed her magic.

----

she heard each and every thought and felt loved.

----

the heart chakra had been hers to command. for the gift that was big mama's, that walter lewis had discovered in his teen age bride, that her children, grand and great-grand accepted easily, as it had always been there, was her enormous capacity to love.

big mama had been a big woman and she had had more than enough love to go around, for anyone, stray children, animals or any soul which needed or was lacking love. big mama always had a saucer or a plate on the stove for the unexpected visitor and always an extra portion of love waiting.

   -come to mama, you can always come talk to mama,

and the minute she'd open those arms and hold you, there could be no doubt that the blessing had begun.

the remarks by clergy, from the two visiting ministers was followed by the singing of *his eye is on the sparrow.*

finally reverend herd stood to delivery the eulogy, he preached,

     -that they the family need not weep and mourn,
       for they had carried their burden well,

and it was time to set it down.

-that the life of mable grey lee bertha fannie anne lou ella
may franklin lewis had been a good one.

-that she had been blessed to have her father with her
until ten years ago when he had left at ninety-seven,

-amen.

-that she had been blessed to be surrounded
by a family that had loved and cared for her
until the very end.
a family that had collectively shouldered the responsibility
that had come after daddy had passed
and she could no longer maintain the house
in cedar green,

and the congregation said

-amen, amen.

-that she had lived to see eleven children to adulthood,
had seen each of them procreate,
had lived to have forty-one grandchildren
and twenty-five great-grandchildren
and nine great-great-grandchildren.
oh, what a blessing it is to be a great-great-grandmother.
-amen, amen, amen!

-that the lord only promises three score and ten years
and anyting past that is bounty.
so to live to be eighty-six is sixteen years
that the lord had blessed her beyond his promise!

and the congregation said again,

-amen.

-to be loved and respected in the community you live,
as evidenced by the turnout this morning,
to know that you are remembered,
what greater thing can a woman ask of her neighbor?

-amen.

-and to depart this life, knowing
that her house was in order with god.
is there no greater glory?

-amen, amen.

-that indeed this was a homegoing celebration
and about that there was no uncertainty.

-amen.
-that this was a time for jubilation and exaltation,
for indeed this good sister was this very day
on the other side of the river jordan,
walking among the saints
and listening to a choir of angels' voices.

-amen, amen, amen!

-that she had been reunited with walter lewis
and all the loved ones she had been separated from during this life,

-amen.

-that she had been recalled to the bosom of the lord,
whom she loved.
could there be any more reason for celebration?

-amen.

-that this was no funeral,
this was a homegoing,
a rejoining,
a replenishing of the body
and a washing of the spirit!

-amen!

-and a cleansing of soul.
a recalling to the seat of glory,
a command performance,
an invitation which can never be refused,
a looking out from the heavenly gates,
for there was no question that mable grey lee bertha
fannie anne lou ella may franklin lewis
was walking in the company of the saints
and at the pleasure of the lord!

-amen, amen, amen!

the right reverend sat down, his work done, the congregation rejoiced, the family was at peace. they had been
reminded of the reasons to celebrate her life. they could feel
her with them. they could feel her blessings. they could feel
her joy.

the congregation listened to the choir sing

-i come to the garden alone,

before the viewing of the body. as from before time, the last
row stood and began the circle line that passed first by the
body to pay last respects and then offered condolences to
those of the family sitting on the front row before they
returned to their seats.

following the benediction, the congregation stood for the
recessional leaving the church. the coffin, proceeded by
flowers, followed by family and congregation was carried out
across the road to the little red mud cemetery.

prayer and the reading of the scripture *ashes to ashes and dust to
dust* comprised the burial ceremony. as the body was lowered
into the ground, it began to snow, ever so gently.

by the time the last flowers have been tossed in, there was a
shimmering over everything.

----

she hovered as she watched the kick dance. a grandson realizing that putting big mama in the ground really meant gone, forever, could not reconcile his loss. throwing himself to the ground, his body convulsed. he kick danced in the red mud and would not be consoled.

she watched her tribe cross the road again returning to the little church for the reception that followed every funeral. the sisters of the congregation had prepared chicken, potato salad, green salad, macaroni and cheese, hot rolls, corn pudding, iced tea and dessert for everyone.

looking down and witnessing her line, all who had come through her, feeling the endless love that she had given unselfishly throughout her life, coming back, tangibly, manyfold, she felt completed.

she would never leave and yet she would never return. not to earth, there was no need. she had earned her wings. she was now ready. she could feel her soul rising. she would remain in heaven.

★ ★ ★

across
for cc

she comes through the fire a spiritwoman possessed,
knocking everything clear, cutting a pathway through the
smoke and tragedy.

she is single thought focused on getting to the babies, those
poor, beautiful babies.

she arrives, a fury.

gathering the new angels in her arms she can hear uncontrollable cries and screams of inconsolable women.

----

sister children's daughters and granddaughters calling from
across the edge of the veil, praying against what they can see
and don't want to believe, asking for release from this cease-
less pain which has taken root within their very souls.

sister children's daughters and granddaughters being held
back, held down, hysterical, screaming what cannot be,

crying and screaming again and again.

                    -oh god, oh god, no! no!

time has stopped.

no seconds tick.

they cannot breathe.

there is no breath, no air.

amid the confusion of flashing lights and sirens, the silences
of babies' cries which will never again be heard and of
mother's wails which will never again be stilled, fill the early
sunday morning.

smoke and the smell of fire snake around neighbors in hasty
morning dress who stand in the unforgiving dawn, surrounding uncontrollable fathers and inconsolable mothers,
knowing there will be no comfort.

life has changed, it will never be the same again.

----

protecting their light souls in her engulfing love, the great
spirit aunt of the eleven month old boy, his three-year-old
cousin, her four-year old brother, their six-year old sister
and their mute twenty-five-year-old aunt ushers them to

the open loving arms and tranquil laps of their waiting ancestors.

-y'all hush now, y'all with family.

the new arrivals take their place.

----

panic awoke sister from a fitful nap. from her sickbed she called to her son so that he could witness as she testified that the babies were all right. the family's babies that had been lost in that terrible fire were all right, they had made it safely across. she had so very clearly seen it in her dream.

★ ★ ★

epilogue

blue pearl
for islah

women in white sat silently singing alongside the shore. ancestral psalms escaped without their notice. softly caressing the waters, their voices carried on the wind into the approaching darkness of this final sunset. neither moon would rise again. the cosmic fire burned lower, casting shadows. soon it would extinguish, signaling the end.

she alone stood and walked the solitary path back to the domed dwelling. she carried all that was left of her civilization, the blue stone. it felt smooth and so alone in her hand.

as she stood before the meditation chamber, her thoughts were drawn to the ship and its passengers slowly moving further and further away from her world. she could still perceive the linking she shared with her mate. she felt his heartbeat pulsing, fainter and fainter, as the distance between them grew to engulf a universe.

as she sat herself down for this final meditation, softly she chanted the syllables passed on from ancestors long silenced. calling upon ancient rites and rituals she gave all she had left before the rumblings beneath her began. if there had been anyone nearby, they would have witnessed the ease of her passing. she had completely disappeared before the cosmic fire burned out.

----

her face remained behind his eyes long after he awakened, as did the sound of the women's lament. in that instant, he remembered all of their lives together and his final promise. across time and the wide expanse of several universes, not only had he remembered, but he had found her.

he woke to find the blue pearl in his hand.

★ ★ ★

About the Author

Theatre artist, author and educator **ihsan bracy** is a graduate of Bennington College in Vermont. He is the author of two plays, <u>Against the Sun, the Southampton Slave Revolt of 1831</u>, and <u>N'toto,</u> a spirit play, as well as two volumes of poetry, <u>cadre</u> and <u>the ubangi files</u>. Twice a CAPS finalist in poetry, he is a former member of the New York State Council on the Arts. **ihsan** has been nominated to the New Renaissance Writers Guild.